Adriana Dana Listeş Pop

# SILVESTRIS ANIMALITERRA AND CARTON MAZEOTOPIA

## MAZEOTOPIA

### SHORT STORIES

Adriana Dana Listeş Pop

# SILVESTRIS ANIMALITERRA AND CARTON MAZEOTOPIA

## SHORT STORIES

Casa Cărţii de Ştiinţă
Cluj-Napoca, 2016

Coperta: Ilustraţiile copertei (coperta I: *Private property*, coperta IV: *Viking House and Alien Ship*)

Editură acreditată CNCS (B)

ISBN:978-606-17-0886-4

*the … the … Vampire.*
*(Why did I hesitate to write the word?)*
*In and out amongst these green hills of what they call here*
*the 'Mittel Land' ran the road, losing itself as it swept round*
*the grassy curve, or was shut out by the straggling ends of*
*pine woods, which here and there ran down the hillsides like*
*tongues of flame.*
*(Bram Stoker, Dracula)*

# PREFACE

This series of short stories were written while living abroad. As in the first volume, *Tongues of Flames and Other Stories*, to make the reading interactive, a series of quotes were inserted: *Theogony. Works and Days* by Hesiod, *The Libray* by Apollodorus, *Argonautica* by Apollonius Rhodius, *Odyssey* by Homer, *Tristia. Ex Ponto* by Publius Ovidius Naso, *The Bible, The New Testament, The History of the Church from Christ to Constantine* by Eusebius, *The Divine Comedy. Inferno* by Dante Alighieri, *The Plum in the Golden Vase* or *The Golden Lotus* by Jing Ping Mei, *Wuthering Heights* by Emily Bronte, *The Scarlet Letter* by Nathaniel Hawthorne, *Dracula* by Bram Stoker, *The Decline of the West* by Oswald Spengler, *In Search of Lost Time* by Marcel Proust, *Spartacus* by Howard Melvin Fast, *The Witches* by Roald Dahl, *Collected Fictions of Jorge Luis Borges, Apollo 13. Technical Air-to-Ground Voice Transcription* by NASA, *Eros and Magic in the Renaissance* by Ioan Petru Culianu, *The Blood of Martyrs: Unintended Consequences of Ancient Violence* by Joyce E. Salisbury, *Constant's New Babylon: The Hyper-architecture of Desire* by Mark Wigley. Readers of all ages are invited to search details about these works online and in the library.

This is a fictional work. Actions, events, names and characters are the creation of the author's imagination. Any similarity or resemblance to actual persons, living or dead, is entirely coincidental.

ADL Pop

# ROVATRIA AND THE DIVINE PURES OF THE HIGH ORDER OF DE RA CULT

*The vampire live on, and cannot die by mere passing of the time, he can flourish when that he can fatten on the blood of the living. Even more, we have seen amongst us that he can even grow younger, that his vital faculties grow strenuous, and seem as though they refresh themselves when his special pabulum is plenty. 'But he cannot flourish without this diet, he eat not as others.*

When I first entered Cette Ringi, the New Babylon, it felt like stepping into a different reality, a dimension left apart from the rest of the world. I touched the secret button on the back of my mobile phone and a blinding light surrounded me, throwing the attackers down to the ground. There, in front of an old, high gate, in Transylvania, the jump was activated in a time node crammed into less than a second. Before the jump, I felt Vlad's presence, telling me that a multidimensional verification has to be done in that particular time-space rift, reported over the centuries to have been an execution place. The attackers got agitated, their anger growing gradually, aroused by the unsuspected ethereal presence. They got hold of me and started to pull me towards them, when I saw Vlad's hologram, projected on the ethereal matter.

The time stopped, people around were casehardened, while Vlad's eyes flashed, inputting information directly into my brain: "This place is charged with unusual energy waves, spectral entities captured you, Rovatria. You can't see them, you are allowed only to sense them, as subtle vibrations, sometimes as a warm or cold tactile sensation on your skin. They are criminals and witches burned here, hundreds of years ago. *A witch is always a woman*, they say. Over time, the Vampires Clan of Dracula used to come here to surreptitiously witness the situation, extract secret thoughts, process them and deliberate. We, the vampires, were the ones to decide which sadistic noble family to punish, which powerful people were involved in commoner's executions. There were noble families renowned for their pleasure in torturing and killing Yobags". "I know, they were enslaved peasants, kept alive in terrible conditions, exploited and tortured for fun, in demonic rituals" I responded. "Yes, some of those nobles were descendants of warlocks that cross-bred humans, led by the demons". "It sounds awful". "Indeed, Rovatria. When their human victims died tortured in horrible agonies, their spirit could have been seen by vampires, capable to read their last memories in less than a second. All this collected historical data is uploaded into these energy sticks hanging in my necklace". I looked at Vlad and I saw a shining necklace, made out of a metallic amalgam of silver, white gold and cosmic matter, on his chest. The necklace appeared to me as a conglomerate of whitish etheric forms, one longer than the other, activated by Vlad when staring at it for more than one second. In that moment, the energy geometrical shapes rearranged into a cross, gaining materiality and metallic consistence.

Sard was responsible with storing and filing the memories in the ethereal archive, updated whenever a relative of a dead victim died, adding new information to the case. Every two hours, a vampiress was supposed to patrol the air in search for fresh information, their flight being organized by Rion. I was told that every vampiress had a special power, tailored for every type of death, coded in a small symbolical tattoo on the inner left arm. Another tattoo was secretly hidden behind their left ear, containing the name of the vampiress, her clan division and a special code for reactivating memories, when attacked by the demons. Rion could scan the information when the vampiress raised her hand towards him, from a few meters away. There were so many of them, and I had the chance to get to know only three of them, called Romphea, Volita and Alis.

Vlad informed me that if I were patient, the chance to meet them all would come. Romphea is a vampiress aged 1600 years old, a playful girl, always smiling and laughing. She has long, wavy blond hair, green eyes shining prankish, a small button-like nose and harmonious teeth, apparent when she smiled. Volita is one hundred years younger, has long dark hair, dark eyes and a cold blooded attitude. Whenever caught by surprise, she smiled peacefully and looked you directly in the eyes. She used to disappear for days into the Tenebrae Silva, the margins of the Tenebrae Dominion, to hide there and hunt, under the protection of the vampires. She was very courageous, nevertheless her enterprise was extremely dangerous.

One day, she came back with a burning sign on her neck, as though branded by the dark spirits. If a warlock had caught her unprotected, she would have been beheaded. Consequently, she would have been obliged to be stay closed into a special vault for a few hundred years, till she could get back to vampirical life. Even though she was not aware of the fact that Rion monitored her escapades, her protective implant emitted signals to the Praetorium, keeping her connected at all times. A group of fighters were sent to prevent her being taken captive by the Tenebrae and tortured for information. She never ventured deep into the Tenebrae Silva, staying at its margins, trying to intercept the data exchanged by the warlocks.

This way, she finds out what humans are targeted by the Tenebrae, information given to Rion, who then would take action to protect the potential victims. Alis is the youngest, a 1200 years old, blue-eyed, blond girl, eager to learn anything would help her evolve into an efficient vampiress. Compared to Romphea and Volita, Alis was only an apprentice, but a clever one, her mind being able to absorb knowledge like a sponge. Although she was the youngest, Alis was a fast learner, breathing into Volita's nape. Each one is responsible for certain deaths, Romphea taking care of the victims of crimes and assassinations, Volita being accountable for suicides, usually prompted by a person or a certain situation, while Alis was responsible for accidental deaths.

"Now take your mobile phone and touch the left upper corner", Vlad told me. When I touched the secret button, I felt absorbed into a time-space fissure. The blinding light dematerialized the organic molecules of my body; flesh and bones, my body vanished, its density being restored, instantly, in a different space.

*There are such beings as vampires, some of us have evidence that they exist*

It was a glass and metal modern building where I was registered, fingerprinted and given an entry card. It was a real office block, part of the earthly reality, a high, square building, covered in black and silver glass panels, reflecting the daylight. Looking towards it from aside, it resembled a huge triangle or a reversed pyramid, perceived from the front side and above, it was clearly shaped as a cube. It was situated near a park landscaped in a forest, around a pond that reflected the sky, important for the water surface. Cette Ringi, the New Babylon dimension was highly secretive, disclosed to only a few workers, called the Auxiliaris. Their cover was a helping attitude, always condescend and supportive, being supposed to activate without payment or other advantages, for a period of time.

Vlad told me that my help was needed there, a centre for lost children, moved away from the EE countries or other parts of the world, in the WE territory. Some of them were hybrids and very few were cross-breeds of ET forms of life. The centre contained two buildings in one, the second one maintained secret, during the night time reconstructing itself in the core, activated by the touch of a button. The light filtrated by the windows was collected in special panels, being used to power the communication satellite, necessary to transmit information by opening the glass veil, which functioned as a roof. It was a colossal, self-sustainable glass box that could set in motion by itself, changing location if required, a smart automatic edifice.

WEEC centre, Western and Eastern Europe Commands, is divided into five floors levelled around the core, each floor having three divisions arranged on the right and on the left side. The reception floor was decorated with a marble mosaic showing a red floral motif. If you looked closely, you could see the red climbing flowers moving slowly, almost imperceptibly, turning into a peaceful dragon. This was possible to see if you were an Auxiliaris, but if you were connected to the Tenebrae, even unintentionally, being used as their host, the flaming dragon could manifest itself as a huge inferno stampa, described by Dante Alligheri in *La Divina Commedia*. The Tenebrae invaded viewer could see the ground beneath opening wide, aspiring him within, in horrible screams. If the individual contemplating the floor was a criminal, the image could have been perceived as falling into an abys where a giant multi-headed dragon was hiding into a river of blood, after an enormous body fluid spill. Terrified, the criminal would feel the blood infiltrating within

1

his shoes, clothes, even skin, climbing up on the legs and body, and would try to wipe it away with the hands. *But fix thine eyes below; for draweth near/The river of blood, within which boiling is/Whoe'er by violence doth injure others;/And I beheld therein a terrible throng/Of serpents, and of such a monstrous kind,/That the remembrance still congeals my blood.* This scenario took place in an imaginary dimension, however the viewer's reactions could be clearly observed.

WEEC was an education centre for human children, hybrids and ET cross-breeds. Some of them were dangerous, practicing forgotten pagan rituals. I saw an ET cross-bred only accidentally, a dark-haired girl, endowed with a pair of unnaturally big eyes, a rather huge head and strong facial bones. I wasn't told her name, and I got scared after her tentative to enter my mind, to implant a shadow. The experience was quite traumatic and the dreams were petrifying in that night. An ET cross-bred child could dive into your mind, the organic intelligence, implant a shadow and destroy important data. I had to be careful and block their entrance into my brain, activating an energy protection, like an invisible helmet around my head. If they had succeeded to get inside, they would have caused irreversible damage to my white and grey matter. Most of the children were hybrids, I could see an imperceptible symbol on their foreheads, a yin-yang circle, rotating continuously, hypnotising you.

Because the Tenebrae attacked and broke their families, their parents were living separately, in different countries. Some of them were born out of wedlock, reason why they had to be kept under surveillance. They developed a double personality and a split mind, part of it frozen at the age when their parents broke up. This was called Bis in Speculo, the second mind being focused on the other parent's wavelength, determining the child's mind to roam into its own infinity. The spatial division enhanced their trauma. The children lived with their families, carers or guardians, most of them cramped into old houses with a single parent, sisters, brothers and a stranger, mom's or dad's partner. This partner could change now and then, leaving space for the hybrids and warlocks to infiltrate and attack the children.

My main mission here was to wait for a reported hybrid to come along, at the same time searching for other data. Vlad communicated me that, according to the latest information, his name was Elbab. He lived trapped in a dematerialized tunnel of dark energy, a projection of a reversed reconstruction of the Tunnel of the Tenebrae, situated underground, serving as a time node. It was a vertical tunnel that connected the Tenebrae with the human dimension, linking it from here, to the cosmic space. I went there to check on it and, amazingly, it looked like a normal house. The vertical tunnel was invisible, nevertheless I was able to see it, staring through a device designed as a double facettes crystal mirror, oriented slightly downwards. The gadget had an energetic electromagnetic field reader and an intelligent core that processed high standards multidimensional information, analysing the data, reshaping its dark spiritual input. Even if it could not be seen with the naked eye, the tunnel was there, projected on the crystal surface, in a reversed position. The ancient tunnel could be felt when getting near the walls of the house, where the air was colder and darker, as if a heavy, undetectable Cortina was drawn around it. After approaching the walls of the house, I instantly felt a powerful headache, forcing me to move away and keep the distance. I left right away, realizing that extra protection was needed for the premises.

*

1

*This then was the Undead home of the King Vampire, to whom so many more were due*

For thousands of years, the vampires' clan of Dracula lived in Transylvania, their historical quarters. They are ethereal beings travelling from deep space, jumping through secret cosmic holes, serving as time-space short-cuts. The vampires hide their offices in the core of the Earth, in a labyrinth of corridors, connecting all the continents, their mapped connection being changed regularly, for safety and protection. In the core of the Earth, there is to be found a secret cosmic base, identical with the other one located in the core of the Universe, mirroring each other as two poles of a cosmic battery. From their base, the vampires can project themselves directly into the Universe, using their minds to jump and travel by setting the destination in their minds. When they are back, it is as if they have dreamt about it. In five seconds, Vlad could travel millions of years light speed distance, accomplish the mission and come back.

Presently in Transylvania, Vlad is a very tall, dark haired, blue eyed man, his straight medium hair covering the ears, partly blocking sound data from entering the brain, like a natural antivirus curtain layer. His mind had undergone the ultimate bio-technological update, being capable to remotely process complete data bases from three different planets, at once. Vlad hides the forehead under another layer of thick, black hair, beneath which the eyes were always looking straight into your face, without a smile. Vlad's eyes are protected by powerful lenses, designed to block undesirable information transfers. Usually, he wears a long black leather jacket, a black tight blouse and black jeans or leather pants. His feet are protected by a pair of black boots, tailored out of a cosmic dragon skin, to reject the Tenebrae's infiltrations, while his hands are covered by special gloves, meant to isolate his energetic signature. He looks around forty, his real age being 40 million years, a cosmic force able to take various shapes and appearances in different interstellar environments. At this point, expressed in human historical chronology, Vlad is presently fighting the warlocks and Mora hybrids, travelling all across Europe.

The earthly base is located in Transylvania, spanning from under the Carpathians, up to the three rivers that pour into the Danube Delta, the three headed Hydra mirroring the identical place in universe, being chosen for a faster data transfer. The three rivers flow and join together at a certain spot, absorbing and purifying the information, finally projecting it on three massive, invisible wheels of energy, rotating above, contrary to the movement of the whirls in the ground waters. The upper wheels of light aspirate the data, encode it and send it away. It is a modest, simple place, to whom nobody would pay particular attention, kept isolated from the rest of the world during history, grasped by violent powers, the last one a hybrid. His human input was greater than the demonical one, but the demon finally woke up inside him to exaggerate control, being cosmically programmed to behave this way. He imposed strict social rules and harsh punishments, trying to elevate his people. Everybody learned to live balanced, eating less, studying and respecting each other, as equals. The instincts were almost eradicated and the time has come for a new project for the whole Eastern European Region, now an elevated stronghold of the Dracula's Clan, preoccupied with extending and purifying the spiritual vibes and clean the territory around their Praetorium.

Why this part of the world and not another one? It is about the Thetis Sea, Achilles' mother and the place of his burial, the White Island, Leuke. Achilles was the greatest

1

ancient warrior, a demi-god, a solar, Apollonian figure, and the embodiment of the purest cosmic energies. His presence can still be felt around, the Omu Peak in the Carpathians being his oldest representation. The legend tells about Achilles the Giant, whose head reached the sky, his feet being washed by the Danube's waves. During historical times, he woke up a few times, shattering the land, then sinking into the Black Sea, where his city awaits for him to come back to life. Ovidius the Poet was sent there by the Roman Emperor, to collect secret data about the Mighty Achilles and his healing waters. *The wealth of so many waters corrupts the waves which it augments, not allowing the sea to keep its own strength.* Ovidius was never able to return where he came from, being buried at Pontus Euxinus, the ancient port of Tomis, near the underground city, taking his secrets into the grave. *When these thoughts steal upon you, absent though I be, I shall be before your eyes as if you had just seen me. And as for me, though I dwell beneath the pivot of the heavens which is ever high above the clear waters, yet I behold you in my heart my only way and often talk with you beneath the icy axle.* He encrypted a few hints into his poems written here in his late years, not entirely decoded, yet. *The letter which you are reading has come to you from that land where the broad Hister adds his waters to the sea.* Achilles was the greatest leader of the Vampires, the founder of the Dracula Clan and the builder of the Praetorium Abyssi Terram.

The vampires were involved in changing history, fuelling Revolutions, fighting for the rights of the common people. They were the mysterious beings that visited Abraham and Lot, and decided to destroy Sodom and Gomorrah. The three men were Vlad, Rion and Sard, appearing to Abraham as three mysterious, divine strangers, sent to check on the bad reports about the two cities. They told Abraham that the claims against Sodom and Gomorrah had reached the cosmic powers, and they were especially sent to verify the situation on the ground. Imagine their shock when the dwellers turned against Lot as a righteous foreigner, and demanded to rape him and his guests, in a collective orgy. The viciousness of the Sodom and Gomorrah's settlers grew so much, that they have turned into wild animals, subjecting everybody to bodily exploitation, to satisfy their own instincts. It was all that seemed to drive and motivate them in life. Seeing this, Vlad, Sard and Rion decided to wipe them off the surface of earth.

They sent the information in space, to the Universal Core, and got the permission to start the physical and spiritual deleting process. The fall of Niniveh was requested for the same reasons - cruelty, injustice and immorality - being labelled by the prophet Nahum *the bloody city, full of lies and robbery*, during the rule of the king Assurbanipal. The Assirians were assured by their god Ashur that their city is impregnable, yet it disappeared for ever. The vampires demanded the fall of the Babylon Empire, at the request of the same prophet: *It is decreed that the city be exiled and carried away.* Babylon Empire was functioning on the same rules, serving the gods of cruelty and physical pleasure, dearest to the king Nabaplausur. The writings on the wall were the divine punishment sign, revealed after the Babylon authorities condemned three children to be closed into a huge flaming furnace, and the prophet Daniel to be put in the den of the hungry lions.

*He can, within his range, direct the elements, the storm, the fog, the thunder, he can command all the meaner things, the rat, and the owl, and the bat, the moth, and the fox, and the wolf, he can grow and become small, and he can at times vanish and come unknown.*

1

To carry on their plan, the vampires had to fight the Tenebrae, their battle being as old as the Universe itself. For a thousand years, the warlocks and the hybrids were allowed to rule Transylvania, where the Praetorium Abyssi Terram is located. Horrible things happened during this block of cosmic time, the power being finally taken back. They were merciless and arrogant, considering themselves superior to all humans, butchered by them whenever they felt like. If there is something the Tenebraes hate, it is certainly morality and normality. It's the worst thing for them, people knowing what's right and what's wrong, for they can control only when ambiguity exists. They feared the vampires, but tried to hunt them one by one, reason why the vampires stick together, two by two, never alone. The main power of the fight moved to America, where the vampires founded a new Praetorium, to watch over the earthly world order. Vampires communicate with each other telepathically and in dreams, sending huge bulks of information in seconds. As the information can be intercepted by the Tenebrae, they have to encode it, using a special brain wave length, while half asleep.

When huge catastrophes happen and many people die at once, a powerful signal is transmitted in the Universe, and a vampire is sent to report on the event. Sometimes, they are expected to erase whole civilizations from the face of the earth, as it happened during the Great Flood, the destruction of Sodom and Gomorrah, the annihilation of Niniveh and the ancient Babylon. Some of those episodes were divine punishments orchestrated by the cosmic powers, many of them remaining, yet, unknown and untold. Even though they are now called vampires, they are ethereal, divine entities, their real name being Divine Pures of the High Order of De Ra Cult. There is a connection with the name of the Sun God Ra, as they are a cult of the Lumen Cosmicam, secret kept by the ancient civilizations, passed on to the Egyptians and the Greeks. It is the pure cosmic light recorded in the Bible that blew away Sodom and Gomorrah, the force of the cosmic ray that blew up that land surface equalling the power of two atomic bombs. The Transylvanian folklore tells us about the Flyers, described as half dead, half alive, powerful forces of the Universe, stronger than the gods - their instruments to fulfil the plans. The plans can change every second, if they are intercepted by the Tenebrae.

The Lumen Cosmicam and the Tenebrae supervise each other at all times, the ability of the Tenebrae being reduced, though. The power of the light cannot be harnessed by the dark, where there is no or very little light, meaning that they cannot see and communicate information at great distances in the Universe. Their powers are limited, however, they excel in luring, tricking humans and hybrids. As demons, they know how to appeal to their instincts and desires. Consequently, their power is greater on Earth and almost absent in the Universe, reason why they prefer to live among humans and use them in every possible way.

Sard is in Britain now, in Western Europe, WE, where a hybrid child was born to Karolina, in a warehouse, being kidnapped by the Tenebrae, immediately. Their millennial target is to create a new Exterminatoris to annihilate humans, to leave only hybrids and warlocks in the world. Sard travels to the major European capitals, being responsible with thwarting the attacks of the Bhara hybrids. Sard's hair is golden like, shimmering in the sunlight, together with his blueish-greenish eyes. He is around 35 million years old, having less than Vlad's millennial experience, the data deposited in his brain being partly earthen. Sard refused to accept protection for his senses, taking the risk of being virused by certain stimuli, convinced he has no reason to fear

2

the Tenebrae. He thinks the Tenebrae have the right to behave in the way they want, taking over whatever they desire, on Earth, even though he gets nervous whenever the humans are hurt, tortured and killed. Sard has just started a secular initiation program in the cosmic power strategies, being instructed in the secrets of the Universe. He likes to wear a black short leather jacket, tight blue jeans and a purple collared shirt, black boots with assorted purple clasp, moulded from titanium, a cosmic information conducting metal, meant to be tracked by the Universal Core of Lumen Cosmicam.

Rion left to USA to watch over the new world order, knowing that the global movement represents a powerful threat to the human reality, present and future, invaded by unknown species of hybrids and warlocks. Rion is around 60 million years old, has got long, blond hair, metallic blue eyes, his protection being hidden at the back of his neck, under the skin. He dresses the same, the drop of colour on the black suit being a diamond which contains detailed information regarding the last hundred million years of cosmic history. The data is accessed directly, downloaded and uploaded whenever he is asked to send it. Soon, I found out that Rion had an unique power hidden in his metallic blue eyes - if he looked at a target, be it person, animal or object, for more than a minute - his eyes would become red, as if in flames, causing spontaneous combustion in a few seconds. During ages, he used to conceal his eyes under a huge, round, black hat. Because of that power, Rion was obliged to hide during daytime, to protect humans from his flame, even though the rumours spread later by the warlocks claimed that he liked to sleep in a coffin, to stay away from the sunlight. I realize now that the figments about him sleeping in the coffin started from the instant combustion abilities and the fiery looks in his eyes.

His eyes are now hidden by special crystal contact lenses, designed to isolate his powerful insight and the ability to start instant combustion. The protection wall can be deactivated when he feels Tenebrae presence nearing from underground. The crystal lenses are connected to the cosmic core of the Lumen Cosmicam, allowing him to see what is happening there in real time.

*The great civilizAtion that is on its way will construct situations and adventures. A science of life is possible. The adventurer seeks out and creates adventures, rather than wait for it to come. The conscious use of environments will condition constantly renewed behaviours. The role of those small flights of chance which we call fate will continue to fade. An architecture, an urban planning and a mood affecting form of plastic expression – the first principles of which exist today – will work in concert toward this end.*

In Cette Ringi, the New Babylon, I was given a house to live in, over one hundred years old, its walls consumed by time and mites, visited by ghosts and shadows. It was a terraced house in a small town, where the WEEC centre was located, flanked by other houses, inhabited by foreigners. There were people from all over the world living here, New Babylon being a different dimension of this world, perceived only by vampires, hybrids and a very few humans. Even though it is spatially situated in this reality, its spiritual blueprint cannot be discerned. The reason is that the Tenebrae created an energetic shield, to block the human's access to their information. The shield looks like a foggy shadow, a subtle grey miasma, floating above people, buildings and in the atmosphere. The only hint I had to sense the shield is the flight of the birds, slightly hardened by the dark energy input, their wings' movement being obviously lagged for less than a second. The shield's strength and density was enhanced by pollution, cigarettes, weed smoke and other emanations.

My mission in Cette Ringi, the New Babylon, was to collect as much information I could find, from every dimension, regarding Obliti Sunt Filii, the Forgotten Children. The haunted house could serve as a source of information from the visiting ghosts, who could know particular things about the town and its history. Some of the haunting spirits have gathered impressive historical data, and are ready to exchange it for diverse services given to them. I was instructed to be careful not to mistake a real ghost with a projection cast by the Tenebrae, meant to mislead me. I was prepared to make exchanges with the ghosts, the vampires providing protection for these situations. Some of the ghosts are mean and hate humans, after being subjected to a painful death, being killed by angry mobs, faithful friends, or even lovers. They want to get revenge and extract your vital energy, then drag you into the other world, before the due time. Rion told me to carry a small symbol moulded in cosmic metal with me, all the time. I also had to upload a string of special active energy coded passwords, to create a spiritual defence around me, let the ghosts know I am protected. Usually, they were able to sense human spiritual blueprint and only if they were filthy evil incarnations, for instance paedophiles, taking advantage of young children, they were branded and terrible plans for their removal from this planet were put into action, on the spot.

The first months in the house were horrible, on the left side I had a warlock neighbour who used to drink, smoke cigarettes and weed, leading an unscrupulous way of life. He was a tall, slim, dark-eyed and dark-haired hybrid, rather ill, roaming during the night under various forms. Evil spirit, he liked to make hideous pranks, breaking into my dreams in the form of a black and white spider, resting above my head, while sleeping, to torment me. I used to wake up terrified after those nights, walking in great difficulty. The bad smell penetrated the left wall of the house, causing terrible headaches, nausea and vomit. It was as if I lived on the edge of hell, bordering all the infernal powers in their abyss of fire and brimstone. *Only DO not leave me in this abyss.* It was the first attack of the Tenebrae upon me, trying to weaken my spirit and make me succumb. When you live in Cette Ringi, the New Babylon, be prepared to face all kinds of awful stimuli, generated by the Tenebrae to torture or tempt you.

In a few days, I comprehended that the houses inhabited by demons, warlocks or hybrids were connected to the Tenebrae Subterraneis, being enveloped into a wall of subtle, infernal, dark steam and smoke, emanated from the Tenebrae's dominion. If I were naïve enough to take the Tenebrae's agents as humans, I would have been lost from the first day. Horrible sounds, yells, beatings could be sometimes heard through the walls where I lived, shaken when the demons tried to break the safety energy layer separating them from the protected humans. So often I have heard the demons jumping on the ceiling and lateral walls, scaring me to death. The Tenebrae's houses functioned as micro-black holes, sucking the volition and the vital energy out of the humans located in their vicinity. The intensity of the manipulation and pressure made on us was unbearable, most of the times. If you weren't strong enough, they could drive you out of your mind, annul your volition, and tantalise you to renounce life, which anyway, seemed aimless and useless in that environment.

When the spider neighbour finally moved, taking all the chaos with him, a new character entered the scene, Lillian. Lillian was a secret hybrid, she had four shadow horns and a key chain that worked as a communication device with the Tenebrae. I checked her molecular constitution during the night, on the street, when her skull could be seen against the moonlight, as if she was a skeleton covered in false skin. She seemed to be a hybrid with a solid demon and warlock structure, trying hard to act human, the mistress of the head of the warlocks, located in UK. Lillian had a dog, a biological replica of a Tenebrae demon, a keeper, a form of Cerberos, the three headed guardian in the realm of the dead. Its name was Cerb; whenever its tail moved, it was transmitting neurologic impulses to Lillian's youngest child's brain, Horpher, causing her to cry in a coded series of sounds, captured by an outer device attached to the pub's door, across the street. The message was multiply coded, allowing the Tenebrae gangs to know what orders they have for narcotics in the next day and sometimes, even commands for prostitutes or organs for transplants, trafficked at hallucinatory prices.

Her human appearance looked in her thirties, a dark-haired woman, her brown eyes rather close on the face, pushed towards a small nose. Lillian's lips were too thin, completely stretched over the rare teeth, yellowed by the cigarette smoke. The woman used to wear tight jeans and a short tight blouse, her belly left visible even when it was cold outside. The first time I saw her, I thought she was a prostitute, having that luring attitude given by too much make-up, her eyebrows being blackened as if outlined by a raw piece of charcoal. It was obvious she wanted to attract attention in an unsubtle way, targeting certain types of men. A former Giver, Lillian was what they call in the New Babylon a Malefactor, a hybrid female belonging to the Dum Incognitum Faciunt, her kids being conceived with various hybrids, warlocks and demon males, who do not take responsibility for their children.

Lillian's children yelled and cried all they long, especially the youngest girl, Horpher, a small demon I kept hearing the mother calling her through the wall. She was a pretty girl around two years old, her blond curls falling down her back like a brooklet. Noisy and rather unhappy, Horpher he was ill with pneumonia, crying hard because her mother went out with the other kids, leaving her at home with a child minder, screaming out in frustration and helplessness. Their big, impure breed dog used to leave faeces in my courtyard, dumping unwanted drugs this way, when police raids were announced in the neighbourhood. Finally, Lillian moved out and had another baby, still not married.

On the right side, the problems started when a new hybrid, a Malefactor, moved in a few months after I settled in. Maia was a blond hybrid with three horns projected as shadows on her head. Imperceptible for other humans, I was able to notice the dark energy horns when she was standing in the sunshine. She had a gardening tool that worked as a special fork, sending data to the Tenebrae. Nobody suspected her, but I have noticed that, when digging the ground, the fork emitted information about particular humans, targeted by the Tenebrae. Her human personality came with two daughters, no husband, and in great moods for loud gatherings. She used to throw big time parties, playing very noisy music, spiced with screaming and fighting, children crying and infuriated guests. Her sister was married to a strange guy, which seemed to be in relationship with both of them. Maia used to smoke the cigarette holding it between two fingers in a defying way, sucking the smoke as the actresses do in the movies, when playing a vicious character. I have heard she is a cardiac and, once, she had a heart attack. However, she does not want to quit smoking, the Tenebrae were tormenting her terribly, it seems. A few months passed,

2

the scandals stopped for a while, Maia got pregnant again and had a new baby, still unmarried.

*I know that ghosts HAVE wandered on Earth.*
*On the other hand, a ghoul is always a male*
*'Speak, woman!' said another voice, coldly and sternly, proceeding from the crowd about the scaffold, 'Speak; and give your child a father!'*

Gradually, I realized that the babies coming out of wedlock was a constant in Cette Ringi, the New Babylon, the females there behaving unreservedly creepy. It was obvious these were the signs of the end. Saddened beyond measure, I couldn't sleep for a few weeks, trying to get in touch with the restless spirits of the night, asking them about the lost women and their children. One of them came to talk to me, a former mother who killed herself after being left in deep disdain, disgraced, unmarried with five children, no food, no money and no roof above their head, in the middle of the 19th century. Her name was Scarlet, she had sad brown eyes, extinct on a bony, wrinkled pale face, her rare, white hair being covered in a white bonnet. Scarlet told me she investigated the situation and found out curious facts. In Cette Ringi, the New Babylon, the society of women is split in three segments, the Malefactor, the Cursores and the Datores. They are all hunted by the hybrids, warlocks and demons, organized in the group called the Dum Incognitum Faciunt, the Anonymous Conceivers, a stronghold of the Tenebrae. They are a vast network of demonical agents, exploiting these women. The Malefactors are usually simple-minded, sentimental women, persuaded to conceive children without being married, directly put without having the guarantee of legal rights for them and their kids. They usually make children after children, using the pregnancy allowance and the child benefit to raise their older kids. Generally, they don't

28

have jobs or money, hope or anything to lean on, their situation being rather disastrous.

The Cursores reject this ruinous scheme and fight for common responsibility, while the Datores are the prostitutes. The Datores have the interest to stop the Malefactor, aiming to use them in their business. At the same time, they try hard to persuade the Cursores to join them. Some of the Malefactor are prostitutes, hoping they get respect if they procreate, thus becoming the perpetual victims of the DIF, Dum Incognitum Faciunt. They move in circles, spinning around their own bodies, without being able to stop, maybe when their fertility comes to an end. The Cursores usually don't want that, they know what's best for them, are clever and fight against the wicked system. Largely, they are highly educated, strong personalities, active and informed. They study, read and practice sports, look quite attractive, healthy and in good shape.

Scarlet told me that Ipha is the leader of the Datores, working closely with Anhel, a transsexual. They travel all the time, being very mobile, afraid they could be found by the vampire or human law enforcement authorities. Scarlet told me that Ipha is a dark-eyed and dark-haired middle-aged woman, the extremely long hair hanging down on her back, like a dead animal. Ipha is in her mid-forties, an old unplaited maiden, waiting for her bridegroom to come, although he never shows up. She has a big, strong nose, rather masculine, a big mouth with fat lips, hiding the uneven teeth, slightly leant outwards, as if trying to bite. Ipha has an unnaturally huge breast, and talks as if she was a small child, taking great joy in imagining she is daddy's baby girl. She also uses wigs and dye to change colour regularly. Together with Anhel and her father, a retired, one-legged bureaucrat, Ipha created a network of the Datores. Their business is based upon an

2

epicurian philosophy of life, outlined by the old disabled, who used to read a lot of books during his life. Ipha attracted around her a lot of superficial, opportunistic men and women, concerned about their looks, hiding physical flaws, using wigs, false lashes, plastic surgery, a collective of snobs. They work together placing girls and boys, women and men to various people, usually rich and powerful, blackmailing them afterwards, managing a dangerous, delinquent enterprise.

*There are the sources and extremities of dark Earth and misty Tartarus, of the undraining sea and the starry heaven, all in order, dismal and dank, that even the gods shudder at; and there are the shining gates and the broNZE threshold, firmly fixed with long roots, made by no craftsman's hand.*

I was warned to never enter a Tenebrae's house, linked to their network of tunnels, built twenty meters into the ground. From what I know, the Tenebrae's tunnels were rudimentary, compared to the vampires' Praetorium, located in the core of the Earth, ceiled into a mixture of diamond, crystal and cosmic particles globe, isolating them from the rest of the planet, especially from the Tenebrae. The huge globe was projected as a shiny, sparkling star-dust, similar to the galactic particles, extended multidimensional, not perceptible to the human and demonical sensory spectrum. The subtle cosmic energy globe was rotating in all directions at the same time, emitting data at incredible speed, in unbelievably high volume to the Universal Core of the Lumen Cosmicam. The amalgam of diamond, crystal and cosmic energy particles were carrying the vampires DNA signature, replicating it wherever it was necessary to intervene, be it on Earth or on another planet. At a signal, the inner Earth cosmic sphere could be dematerialized and transferred to the Universal Core, in case the Tenebrae would invade it to put hands on their massive collection of cosmic information.

- Why is it dangerous? They wouldn't know what to do with it, I asked Vlad.

- They could break the codes, in the end, and use the data to upgrade their DNA, situation which would enable them to evolve, manage the power of Lumen Cosmicam, getting more dangerous than ever.

- Where is Tenebrae's dominion?

- You will see it tonight, in your dream. I am going to take you there.

- Can they sense us, Vlad?

- No, they can't, we are sealed into a micro-molecular light tube. We are present as *de lumine*, a few photons. We are still part of the darkness for their sensory organs. They don't have the proper mental technology, the accurate organic intelligence strategy to even suspect our presence here.

Tenebrae Subterraneis was a network of dark, constricted tunnels, artificially lit and alpha-numerically ordered, where the miserable dead souls were jam-packed into metallic cages, every one of them being given a code number, representing their spatial location in the network and their ethical file, containing a detailed list of sins and crucial mistakes. The dead souls were called to daily torments and punishments, organized in four shifts, not being allowed to rest at all, forced as they were to listen to the other's inconsolable screaming and crying. Regularly, a stream of lava and boiling blood, where crushed body members and blasted internal organs were floating within, was directed towards them, four times a day, drowning everything in its way. Above the river of blood, groups of almost naked women danced languorously, calling their names and code numbers. After the dance, a viscous, cold darkness fell over the dead souls, moment when invisible, giant worms, leaches and tentacular beings constituted of dark energy crawled on their skins, sucking their vital energy, feeding on their fear and awe. The blood was collected and conducted through a series of red and black pipes, the red ones absorbing and pouring the mixture of blood and lava, while two large black pipes aspirated the body parts. The vision was truly horrible and I could never forget it, not till Vlad completely erased it from my memory.

*Who is not acquainted with those cohorts of demons of Christianity whose most benign activity was continually to exert natural constraints (drowsiness, hunger, erotic desire) upon people conceited enough to think themselves above them?*

A few days later, Rion informed me that fatherless and motherless babies are nests for the Tenebrae, the demons feeding on their poor spirit and unhappiness. The demons called incubus and succubus torment them and their mothers, their minds being used as hosts, dreadful tactics being prepared for the weakest of them. Every Malefactor has an incubus or succubus feeding on her vital force, which can be seen as a subtle mist around the victim's eyes, the glimmer of light being faded away. The demons encourage their victims to drink, take drugs and fornicate, to extract their vital energy, being attracted by the smell of cigarettes, alcohol and weed. If you looked harder, you would see the air blurring around the victims, like small vortexes. Rion informed me that, for this reason, in the former communist countries, couples were not allowed to conceive children out of wedlock. The warlocks couldn't stand it and tried to overthrow the regime, undermining it by creating secret networks of Dum Incognitum Faciunt, obsessed with luring human females, to impregnate them. Then they used them, the mothers and the babies, tormenting them in every way, making them the most wretched creatures on Earth. It seems it had nothing to do with the political regime, this being just a mere reflection of the spiritual fight led across the universe. If not baptized, the nest babies could become monsters, responsible with killing large numbers of people, in staged events. The Tenebrae's main goal is to exterminate humans using unbaptized, hybrid babies. Kidnapped at their birth, the Tenebrae can avoid the Christian baptizing, thus raising them according to their demonical rites.

Sard located himself in UK, trying to find Elbab, Karolina's child taken from her at childbirth, during a working day in a warehouse. In Cette Ringi, the New Babylon, demonical hybrids and warlocks always infiltrate and tend to torment and exterminate humans. It is then that the Divine Pures get the message across and send a vampire to investigate and eliminate the cause. The balance of the earthly world must be established again, as it interferes with the Cosmic Order, being a battle fought every second. The power of the Tenebrae was greatest in the ancient times, conserved till early Christianity, when some heretical sects worshiped the fallen wisdom and abolished the law and the real father. The fallen wisdom was called Sophia, and there was an ignorant demiurge accused for all the problems in the world. The sects were built on heresy, Paul of Samosata believed in trinity and Monarchianism, preaching adoptionism. He was criticized by the Church for the orgiastic cult created, leading a dirty life, worn in swings and orgies, especially on New Year's Eve. His people were called *payl*, the dirty ones. Another sect was that of Messalians from Edessa, accused of not practising marriage, neglect of their children, sexual promiscuity and even sexual mutilation.

*Have you seen that awful den of hellish infamy, with the very moonlight alive with grisly shapes, and every speck of dust that whirls in the wind a devouring monster in embryo? Have you felt the Vampire's lips upon your throat?*

3

Vlad appeared near me one day, materializing out of an energy cloud, scattering in my room.

- Your help is needed, urgently, Rovatria. Come with me.
- Where are we going, Vlad?
- We found Elbab.

He surrounded me in a glittering cloud and we disappeared, reappearing immediately in the desert.

- Elbab had suffered some accelerated, unexpected mutations, turning into a hideous monster, hidden by the Tenebrae in their dominion, connected to the Earth's surface through the Tenebrae Silva. In the meantime, their army is being raised, served by the Dum Incognitum Faciunt, taking aim to destroy the world in just a few days. Their plans got out of control, counting on the assistance of a cruel alien race, from a distant planet.
- Who are they, Vlad?
- They are the ones who planted hybrids on Earth long time ago, a breed of partly extra-terrestrial, partly human mutants. Some of them have Arthropod Phylum exoskeleton and constitution. I was there when they arrived on Earth. It was an outpour of dark matter, a kind of black plasma in the desert, during a solar eclipse. The dark plasma fed on the sand, melting it instantly, absorbing and transforming it into an unknown form of energy, expanding more and more, till it reached the size of a big city. Then, they materialized out of the dark matter, taking shape, one by one, together with their ship. That dark plasma can exist in liquid state, mentally controlled to become matter in any condition known on Earth. When getting in contact with earthly matter, they can take any form they want, be it vegetal, animal, human or artificial. Touching the sandy ground, the black plasma extended over colonies of humans, spiders, scorpions and

other desert arachnids, small insects, plastic recipients, metallic remains of crashed planes and all kind of rubbish.

Vlad explained that the extra-terrestrial plasmatic entities could make themselves invisible, absorbing the earthly matter, at the same time allowing to be absorbed. More than that, they could enter human bodies, without even being suspected. Once inside humans, they could prompt them to do whatever they wanted, meeting absolutely no resistance. Generally, the invisible aliens weren't aggressive towards humans, they just invaded them, using them for their own purposes. Actually, they located themselves into human minds, causing slight mutations in the physical appearance, as well as gradual changes in the way of thinking and in the behaviour. The last stage of the process is the reproduction, when the aliens pass their genes to the new born children, who would be aliens in human aspect, completely subordinated to the extra-terrestrial forces. The terrifying fact was that the extra-terrestrial plasmatic hybrid children had the ability to grow in three days as others in three years, reaching the maturity age in less than a month, being capable to reproduce at that stage. Hence, in a few years, the whole Earth could be invaded by mutant alien breed, the human race risking to be completely replaced or wiped out, and the consequences would be disastrous, impossible for humans to even grasp it. The last mission of the vampires was the most challenging, for many thousands of earthly chronological years running out on this planet.

*To be continued*

# SILVESTRIS ANIMALITERRA

Silvestris is a mysterious land where Animaliterra, the Territory of Animals, is located. After the Flood, all the animals on the Ark decided they must break free from the human oppression. They summoned all the faunae to a debate if they wish to remain with the humankind or leave to subsist independently. The discussions were animated, impassioned and antagonistic, fatalities being registered on each side. Those wishing to remain were called traitors and were subjected to several assassination attempts. Some of them succeeded, some of them did not, and since then, a few species became extinct. This is the case of the fantastic animals recorded by the Stone Age artists in the caves. The other side of the social-political debate was represented by the leave supporters, quite violent in their endeavour to extract the animals from the human influence and exploitation.

One day, I was attacked by a gang of criminals, while trying to park the car downtown. They stole my car and kidnapped me, keeping me hidden in the back of a truck, hands tied, head in a sack. It seemed an eternity. It was dark, humid and stinky. After a while, I don't know if it was a few minutes, a couple of hours, weeks or months, they deserted me in Silvestris Animaliterra. It was a dense, obscure jungle with huge trees and vicious animals, where I had to survive by all means, all alone, lost in the woods, me against the most voracious beasts that ever existed on Earth. After a few days, I realized that Silvestris Animaliterra is an island surrounded by waters, where no human has ever set foot, Animaliterra being absent from our maps, it cannot be seen even on GPS. I really don't know if it is located on Earth or on another planet, everything is different there. The water is red, almost bloody, the sky is always cloudy, smothered by ponderous, ashen clouds. When it rains, it starts a terrible outpour of ashes and coals powder.

The trees grow upside down, with their roots out. No green leaves, no flowers, no butterflies. The animals are hideous, a mixture of animals, insects and humans. Rarely, some of the monsters develop vegetal traits, for instance huge, purple maize husks instead of ears, tree branches as an alternative to noses, nuts as a substitute for eyes. Big, horrifying spiders carrying tiny human heads, endless poisonous snakes with multiple legs, rats with potato eyes, big bugs with hooves, an atrocious breed of toxic wasps and hideous mice. It was awful to look at them, unbearable. Terrifying nightmares tormented me during the nights, and I must confess it took a long time to understand those weren't dreams, but real events. However, my mind was so shocked that couldn't accept it. I had to hide in plain sight, in a modest hut constructed with fresh maize husks, daily, a few of them being enough to build a comfortable hut, Animaliterra maize being huge, without knowing for sure if it was poisonous or carnivorous.

Sometimes, it released a strange smell, resembling the toxic chemical used in the plastic factories. If the maize leaves were dry, the animals would have noticed me, immediately. After a couple of weeks, I befriended a peaceful creature, half dog, half hen, cackling all day long around me, to cover my presence. Its name was Cackeroodoo, a joyous animal, entertaining me with its tittle-tattle, helping me forget about home. Of course, its constant chatter and giggle drove me crazy sometimes, situation which required the use of ear plugs, to stifle the noise. In time, I learned its language, succeeding to communicate in signs, gestures and onomatopoeias. Cackeroodoo told me, somehow, barking and cackling, that the leader of Silvestris Animaliterra is a horned, furred hippopotamus, called Hippomanes. Descending from the antediluvian fauna, Hippomanes, mammoth sized, used to defend its territory ferociously.

I saw him one day, from a safe distance, a horrible half gorilla, half hippopotamus monster, with two tarantulas instead of eyes. He rules in terror. Every animal looking straight into his eyes is immediately seized by his personal guards, tortured and killed. Hippomanes couldn't stand anybody see his eyes, two hairy, fat Theraphosidae, moving their tentacles synchronously. Frightened, the animals resorted to terrible solutions, some of them removing their eyes. Alarmed, the great majority of population pretended they were blind, keeping their eyes covered with patches of rat fur, trying to protect their lives and save their families this way. Cackaroodoo made me promise I would keep away from Hippomanes, avoiding his eyes. How could I ignore his advice when the mutilated dead bodies of the naïve, misinformed or defiant animals were rotting at every corner of the island?

One day, the girl Hippomanes was in love with, lately, disappeared and he grew awfully angry, wreaking havoc on the island. All the animals ran away in horror, hiding deep under the waters, in caves, under the ground or high above. I and Cackaroodoo remained in our maize hut, counting on the fact that nobody knew about our existence. Hippomanes sent guards to search for the girl, while he was looking for her everywhere, too. Suddenly, we heard noise around our hut. Cackaroodoo went out to see what's happening, when it saw Hippomanes standing up, growling harshly. Two huge curved tusks got out of his mouth, stabbing the air upwards, blood-stained, with strips of raw flesh hanging off the two metres long tusks. Hippomanes was four metres high, his shoulders very wide, around two metres. He had fists as big as boulders, being able to crush everything in his way, especially when he was furious. The head was round and hideous, close to the size of a tractor wheel, on which the tarantulas were fixed towards our hut, agitated. Hippomanes took the hut in one claw, finding us within, trembling with fear. He snatched us in his left fist and started a wrathful run, jumping over the trees and rivers, roaring terribly. I fainted, together with Cackeroodoo, while rocking inside Hippomanes' fist, bumping my head against his thumb, stiff as stone. Cackeroodoo kept wining and weeping till it fell asleep, sobbing.

When we came back into our senses, we found ourselves in a rudimentary cage, built out of strong, irregular tree branches put together. First, we thought it is a good thing the bars are vegetal, but studying it, we realized the wood pulp was different, a mutant, metallic one. All our hopes went down the slope, when somebody came to transport us somewhere else. For three days, we were kept in the middle of the town, for every animal to come and spit on us, laughing, throwing garbage towards us, fart in our direction or any other crazy action could cross an ante-diluvian animal's mind. They didn't feed us at all, leaving us the only option to eat what was thrown into our cage, if we were lucky enough. Cackeroodoo had a few friends, who came every day to call us various names, like "little piece of shit", "mother buckers", "nomads" or anything more offensive to divert attention from the food wrapped in dirty, slimy leaves, catapulted inside our cage with a sling.

Hairy, half vegetal, half fleshy rotten tomatoes splashed on our faces, letting the stinky juice dribble down our cheeks, into the mouths. The squashed tomatoes were then picked up,

3

eaten raw in great hurry. Eggs with small grown wings and chicken claws, huge microbes and bacteria as big as an apple or a melon, bloody red onions, giant carrots with eyes and moustaches were among our menu those days, served unwashed, altered and unhygienic, with curses, insults and humiliation. After three days and nights, our cage was fixed on the back of a giant dinosaur bird with carnivorous vegetal-fleshy ropes that could cackle and laugh maleficently in our faces. Cackeroodoo was shivering terribly, crying and screaming horribly in the darkness, while I tried to comfort him, unsuccessfully, though. He was inconsolable, pray to a horrifying state of mind that cannot be described in words. The only solution was to hit his head against the bars, regularly, till he lost his counsciousness, again, to have a bit of silence that could allow me to think.

It was pitch dark, although the powerful lightnings setting the sky on fire permitted me to see the dinosaur bird was carrying us above a marsh land, teeming with giant worms, leeches and snakes, raising their tentacles up towards us, to crash the dinosaur bird and make us their pray. Here and there, a rudimentary mud tower was erected, leaning aside, almost falling apart. The mud towers belonged to the army leaders of Hippomanes, the cruellest creatures on the island. For their state of evolution, the mud towers were the latest technology, the owners being very proud of their residence. Every mud tower was guarded by a dragon spitting fire, roaring dreadfully. The dinosaur bird started to descend on a rocky cliff near a black ocean, in a thick darkness, when Cackaroodoo woke up, massaging its head, sighing.

· Where are we now? Cackaroodo asked, barking and cackling.

· I don't know, it seems to be by the seaside or near an ocean shore. The water appears to be black.

40

- Oh, it is the end of the world, the Black Waters. We are doomed. It's worse than death, said Cackaroodoo, starting to sob hysterically.

- What is worse than death? Cackaroodoo, tell me, please. Stop sobbing, I need information to set up a survival plan.

- Ohhhhh, ohhhhhh, there is no chance of survival here, we will die in a few minutes, said Cackaroodoo.

- Will they torture and kill us?

- Every living creature, small or big, wants to kill and eat us.

- How do you know?

- There is a legend about the Black Waters, the place where the most dangerous villains are deserted. Nobody ever escaped, although they say there is an enigmatic hero here, helping the convicts to make it alive in an unknown place. Some legends say the hero is a forgotten god or divine warrior, worshipped before the Flood. He educates the doomed, teaching them how to work the land, carve the wood and some other useful things.

- This sounds good, it could be our only chance.

- Yes, but it could be unreal, I don't know ...

Cackaroodoo fell into a prolonged silence, displaying a bitter face, its mouth frozen in a ridiculous rictus. I left him to go on staring in the darkness, while feeling the rock under me with the hands, trying to find out where we are. It was warm, almost hot, and the black waters were steaming, spreading a rotten smell around. It was as if dead animal bodies were boiled in a giant pot, by a wicked, ugly witch. When trying to take a step towards the water, monsters started to roar, making our hair stand on its ends. I stopped right there, trying hard to remain still.

- What are you doing, are you out of your mind? Cackaroodoo yelled in panic. Sit still, will you?

- Why?

- Monsters are in alert now, they know we are here.

Crocodiles, huge snakes and balaurs were closing from every direction, roaring deafeningly. A giant half dragon – half dinosaur with a hideous tortoise shell on its belly poured burning flames and lava on us. If we didn't avoid their fire, we would have been turned into ashes in just a few seconds. To escape the certain death through burning, me and Cackeroodoo jumped into the Black Waters, without looking back, yelling desperately. Huge crocodiles with fangs, covered in cast iron spices, hassled us, together with an odd breed of pre-historic rhinos enclosed in steel fish scales, endowed with huge horns, as big as the street light poles. When we were about to be stabbed in the face by a rhino's horrifying horn, some strange ship or submarine surfaced, opening a trap, letting us in. It was as if God himself came to save us and we felt very indebted to our savour.

We couldn't see him. All we could discern was a long gangway leading to a dark tunnel. We walked that way, urging each other to take the first step, being scared of what might happen next. Cackaroodoo was trembling with fear, without being able to utter a single word. He only closed his eyes, refusing to open them anymore, terrified he would see awful monsters again. Actually, it was all we could be sure of, a succession of an endless series of atrocious monsters, came out of the wildest imagination, truly unconceivable. Nevertheless, they were lurking around, waiting to jump in front of us, like in a horror movie that never ends. It was me who took the initiative and made the first move towards the tunnel, it was impossible to ask Cackeroodoo to do it, he was completely overwhelmed. And who could blame him? He was just a simple half hen-half dog peaceful being, preoccupied to lay a furry, toothy egg, dreaming of a pleasing bone in return.

42

Holding Cackeroodoo, I stepped into the dark, stinky tunnel. My feet were shaking, as if walking on water. It was pitch dark and we couldn't see anything first, but gradually, our eyes got used to the complete lack of light and probably because of the fear and horror, I thought I can see a bit, even though I am not sure it wasn't a repugnant illusion. I heard a swish above our heads, on the tunnel's ceiling and I looked up, where a huge black spider was covering all the ceiling with its hairy body and legs, from one end to the other. The spider had eyes all over its body which seemed to be designed in sharp corners and miss-matched patches of Arachnida material. It appeared to me as a terrible nightmare, its body composed of a community of spiders, all rearranged in a single motionless body, ready to attack as one, at a signal. "Where is the web? Where is the web?" I mumbled, but I could hardly move my lips. I was paralysed. I forgot about Cackaroodoo and Hippomanes, the mutant dragons and other threats, incapable of moving. I wasn't sure I was awake or asleep, maybe dead. Cackaroodoo realized I stood still, and yelling, grabbed my hand and started to bite it, intending to wake me up, without result. Then he dragged me after him, crying and screaming.

· Wake up, wake up, we are going to dieeeeeeee! Cackaroodoo cried out, biting my hand up to the shoulder.

Feeling his teeth in my flesh, I woke up, understanding where we were. I refused to look up to see the giant Arachnida above, trying to trick my brain to move a few metres. The arm was hanging useless, bloody and torn into pieces, and my first thought was to get out of the tunnel, be out of the giant spider's reach. One could smell a terrible stench, as if thousands cadavers were lying in the sunshine, rotting. I took a few steps, consuming huge amounts of physical energy, when a giant octopus appeared in front of us, its tentacles spread on the floor, flickering in the filthy, foul water, which seemed to reach our abdomens. Giant spider above, unimaginably big octopus beneath our feet, it was considerably overwhelming to face so many appalling dangers, concomitantly.

When we thought there is nothing else we could do to save ourselves, a blinding light flashed out of nowhere and something like a mechanical insect-robot grabbed us and took off, two fingers distance from the terrifying spider. The Arachnida opened a disgustingly hideous mouth showing innumerable sharp teeth, ready to swallow us, when the insect-robot cut it with a metallic tool, designed as a fork with twelve tusks. With a terrible roar, the enormous spider broke into countless small and medium sized spiders, running scared on the tunnel's ceiling. Some of them fell down on us, making me and Cackaroodoo shriek and jump hysterically. The mechanical insect sprayed us with a strong water shower, to clear the myriad of arachnids. When hit by the burst, the innumerable spiders screamed awfully, writhing, growing mad women's bodies and heads, with tentacle hair standing on its ends, dyed purple, reddish, blond or dark, laughing maleficently. The hair was either much too long, reaching their feet, or too messy, displaying an imperturbable calm, frozen smile, as if a picture was stuck on their faces.

We lost our consciousness and the mechanical insect carried us out of the tunnel. A powerful light made me come back into my senses. We were in a circular ship, together with a tall, middle aged man. His head reached the ceiling, where a stream of fresh oxygen was released into the atmosphere by a pump. I and Cackaroodoo were breathing through special masks. We found out later that we were deep under water, in a submarine, equipped with cutting edge technology, as well as small garden where all kinds of fruit and vegetables were glowing, constantly fed with fresh water and artificial solar light.

-You don't need your masks into the garden, the tall man said. Don't worry, I know your story, I will take you back home, in no time. You should rest now.

When I woke up, there I was in the car, parked in my own courtyard, as if nothing had ever happened. Utterly relieved, I rushed inside, immediately starting to write the disturbing adventures experienced in Silvestris Animaliterra, publishing the texts, serially, in a multilingual cultural magazine, striving to make it pass as a delirious speech, scribbled by an unexperienced paper scratcher.

# CARTON MAZEOTOPIA

Massy Carton Mazeotopia is a cellulose dimension where carton people live. They have rectangular bodies of various sizes, made out of beige cardboard produced in a multistage process. It starts with dissolving raw materials into water, mechanically cleaned to remove impurities, followed by heating up to 95 degrees for pasteurization and disperging. Then it comes the wet end stage, wet press section, drying and coating section. The final products are cut from a big cardboard Tambour, according to the customers' orders. When not sleeping on the huge, long shelves, the cartons grow hands, feet and sometimes heads that help them get off the shelves and land on Wooed 'n Lets Play! carried by automated mechanical vehicle-beings called Lolly Woops. The Lolly Woops are happy moving around in the huge maze constituted of linked aisles organized in an innumerable number of tall shelves. The cartons' most cherished desire is to be able to leave the shelf and be delivered to a client, it even doesn't matter to whom, at all. The carton people and the Lolly Woops are led by a system Oh, Why Me Sleep!, generating commands and operating the movement of the carton people from one coordinate to another.

When the system calls their code number registered in a certain position, the cartons wake up, confirm their position, activate their superior and inferior members together with their heads and jump off the shelf on the Wooed 'n Lets Play!. The Lolly Woops are prepared to receive them, between seventy and two hundred per hour. The cartons arrange themselves on the wooden surface one above the other, bumbling and mumbling, climbing on each other, fighting and arguing, pushing each other around. They manage to finally stack themselves chaotically, pressing on those firmly caught down under, supporting the heavy weight of the ones above, till they reach a two meters height, at the most. In order to keep them together and isolate them from reality, a thin film or plastic membrane, clear or coloured, is wrapped around them in great speed, maintaining the exterior world out of reach. Close to each other, stuck to their own reality, put to sleep again, the cartons are transported by Lolly Woops to the loading bay area, where the stacked and foiled Wooed 'n Lets Play are expected by the Try Lars to be taken away, nobody really knows where.

The Wooed 'n Lets Play! are carried by the Lolly Woops through a complicated labyrinth of corridors, aisles and pathways, to lose their way. The carton people are not allowed to retain their way towards the Try Lars, it would enable them to find their way back. To keep them engaged in a half sleep, half awake state of mind, the system plays music all the time, feeding it to their left or right ear through a headset. Every time the cartons must be put to sleep, the system commands "sleep", and when the system requires waking up, it utters the command "wake up". The system even tells them "good night", and the cartons can choose the type of voice they like – female or male - and several languages to operate in their ears. Every carton knows its position on the shelves, automatically generated by the system in a series of combined digits starting from 0 to 9. Sleeping on their shelves, the cartons have to confirm their position now and then, saying their digit code comprising the aisle number, the shelf number and its floor, as the shelves are very tall, up to a very high ceiling. Cartons could get confused by the fact that there is a number one digit put in front of every aisle and shelf number, making it difficult to make the confirmation. Whenever are allowed to stay awake, the cartons walk aimlessly among the isles, mumbling a long string of ciphers combined with letters, half asleep, acting like an odd type of carton zombies.

One day, a newly received and stocked carton seemed to behave strangely. Cartonda no. 140 128 09 75 couldn't go to sleep all day long, ruminating secret thoughts instead. Cartonda got tired sleeping on the designated shelf, preferring to watch what the other cartons were doing. Cartonraw, an old carton, forgotten on a dusty corner of the same shelf, realized Cartonda was restless, trying to figure out what's going on in Massy Mazeotopia. He saw that Cartonda's hands, feet and head kept coming out while resting on the shelf, which was quite unusual for its situation. More than that, Cartonda used to whisper all kinds of words and songs to itself, thinking that nobody else can hear it. Amazed, Cartonraw called him from three positions above:

- Hey, Junior, keep silent!
- Who is there? Aren't you asleep, like the others?
- No, as a matter of fact, I am not sleeping. Why do you care?
- Don't get wild, Pops, I am not trying to act funny. I can't sleep.
- Why?
- I think it is a fabrication error or something.
- Maybe. In my situation, it started after a few years of sitting still on this miserable shelf. First, I thought it is a dust allergy, but then I realized it is the waiting process.
- You got tired of waiting, lost your patience.
- Yeah, something like that, I think it is a kind of a mysterious disease.

· Oh, I don't know … In my case, it is not an illness, maybe a psychological condition. I keep worrying about the robustness of the metal shelves are made of. What if they begin to rust and cede, taking us all to the floor?

· You are not allowed to worry, don't let yourself be concerned with what happens around, the system will sense you and it might want to get rid of you.

· How comes?

· The cartons have to be happy, displaying a positive attitude and a complete trust in the system, it knows it all. Don't bother with anything else, just sit there, snoozing or day dreaming about wonderful things or merely common-sense, achievable desires, like the rest of us…

Cartonraw fell asleep instantly and Cartonda remained silent, thinking about what the discussion. "Achievable dreams…. Hmmmmm, what is that, I wonder" thought Cartonda, aware of his position on the fourth row of the shelf, slightly oriented to the left, at the maximum height, except the ones hanging above, on the top of the shelves. Pretending to sleep, Cartonda watched what was happening around. The system started to move Cartonda on different shelves, the rule being to never leave a carton on the same shelf for more than two weeks, to create bonds with the ones around. In less than three years, Cartonda realized Mazeotopia had ninety aisles, every aisle starting from one hundred to approximately five hundred positions. Removed from the fourth shelf for one hundred times, then on the third for two hundred times, going on the fifth for a change, wherefrom he fell down, bending his right corner.

When he returned on the fourth shelf located in a different aisle, Cartonda saw a glossy carton near him. He studied her closely, noticing that whenever waking up to confirm position, Cartongi grew nice hands, feet and a very

4

long horsy hair on its head. When Cartonda tried to talk to Cartongi Horsy, got no answer, she didn't seem aware of her position in Mazeotopia, being asleep or in a numb state of mind. Cartonda was curious what was she dreaming while napping, observing multiple bar codes floating above, where the head appears when she is awaken. "Oh, she is dreaming to be sent away to a client. What a waste of time and energy...". Cartonda was disappointed to understand that Cartongi Horsy's greatest desire was to meet the needs of an ordering client. "This isn't a dream, this is a nightmare", Cartonda told himself, bitterly disappointed. In a few days, Cartonraw landed right near Cartonda, just three positions away from Cartongi Horsy to the left.

- Hey, Pops, you're back again. Right on time, Cartonda told him.

- Yeah, had enough of it, only sleepers everywhere, nobody to chit-chat. Not a chance.

- Aha, here I am, ready to report. Take a look to the left, old man. See what I mean?

- The glossy one?

- Yeah, what do you think?

- She is a commoner. Sleeping beauty, not enough brain to stay awake.

- I noticed she is not a genius, but she seems cute. She dreams to be delivered to a client.

- They all do, and the client never comes or buys them and sends them back again, claiming the refund.

- Saying they are faulty. And the client is always right, you know what I mean...

- Unfortunately, he is.

- Well, then the returned cartons are given a lower position on the shelf, till they are made redundant.

- What happens to them in that situation?

- They are sent to recycling premises.
- Tough luck.
- It is.
- What can we do to help her?
- Nothing. I advise you to not interfere, it is dangerous.
- Why?
- You could fall off the shelf, damage yourself. You would be sent to recycling right away.
- Ouch, it is not pleasant to picture it.
- Not at all.
- I will think of something, nothing else left to do all day long.
- I must go to sleep now, save energy for rainy days.
- Sleep tight.

Cartonda believed that escaping Mazeotopia would allow him to live a thrilling life, lying down on a dusty shelf for days and weeks was not funny. He developed some unknown types of allergies and a nervous condition, getting irritable, grumpy, negative and quarrelsome. One afternoon, Cartonda noticed a Lolly Woop was heading towards his aisle, coming his position. The carton felt a profound emotion; growing somehow enthusiastic, his head, hands and feet started to appear, together with a reserved smile on his face. It was his opportunity to escape, long thought of, lately. Maybe this Lolly Woop would make a transport to the Try Lars, and he could escape. The Lolly Woop stopped right in front of his position, while the system started to call cartons' code numbers. One by one, the cartons confirmed awakening and landed on the Wooed 'n Let's Play!. A big riot began, the cartons pushing, swearing, cursing and hitting each other. They all got wild, finally rearranging themselves in an almost ordered pile of cardboard, although a bit chaotically. When he heard Cartongi Horsy's code, Cartonda's smile froze.

Cartongi confirmed awakening with a broad smile, her dream – to be delivered to a client - was about to come through. Cartonda had to do something about it.

- Pops, it is the glossy one. She is being ordered. Help is needed, wake up...!
- Oaaaaahhhh, Caartonraw yawned, I am too tired and old for this business...
- Pops, she will be sent back, ending up at recycling.
- Ok, ok, when I say three, we jump on the Wooed 'n Let's Play! Be prepared!
- You bet I will...

Cartonraw pronounced number three and both of them jumped above the Wooed 'n Let's Play!. Caartonda rolled aside dangerously, hitting Cartongi Horsy, threatening to fall down from the top of the Wooed 'n Let's Play!. Cartongi screamed, terribly scared.

- Hey, tough guy, are you crazy? Do you want to kill me?
- Oh, no ... Sorry, my bad.
- You should be. It is my big day, today. I am being ordered by a client. I am so happy. Am I glossy enough, what do you think?
- Yes, you are, try to stay awake. The system will put us to sleep again in a few seconds.
- I feel heavy-eyed, already, Cartongi said, feeling her eyelashes hefty.
- Sweetie, be alert, things are starting to move in an unknown direction. You need to be awake.

The system said "Good night" and all the cartons fell asleep, except Cartonda. The Lolly Whoop got out of the aisle, traveling on the main corridor, headed for the Try Lars bay area. Cartonda had to think quickly, at the same time memorizing the route from his aisle and shelf to the Try Lars, a valuable piece of information he could certainly use, at the right time. Cartonda counted thirty aisles straight ahead, ten more to the right and the bay area was there, in front of his eyes. "Wowwww, now we're going places" said Cartonda, enlarging his eyes. The bay area was wide, teeming with Lolly Woops, Fourkey Leefty, Richy Trickies and other mechanical entities he wasn't aware of, before. They all moved in great speed, delivering and loading Wooed 'n Let's Plays!, moving them in every direction. It was a busy zone, quite contrary to the quiet aisles region, where everybody slept. It was one in a life-time chance for Cartonda to see this. He yahoooed once, overwhelmed with happiness, but stopped immediately, he could reveal himself and get into trouble. On top of the Wooed 'n Let's Play!, he could easily be seen by anybody. Cartonda closed his eyes, freezing instantly in an uncomfortable position which could enable him peep around now and then. In the next minute, they were taken to the Try Lars and Cartonda couldn't hold his shout of joy. In a few seconds, his Wooed 'n Let's Play! was inside the Try Lar. It was hot and shady inside, stuck together with other Wooed 'n Let's Play!, around twenty six, thirteen on one side, thirteen on the other side. A huge mechanical drone equipped with microphone, camera and mobile communication was overflying, monitoring cartons' suspect movements. Cartonda pretended he is dead, no breathing, no blinking, no nothing. Suddenly, the heavy metallic gates closed with a thundering noise. The Try Lar was moving now, Cartonda could breathe and jump for joy. Hearing the outpour of happiness, Cartonraw woke up, startled.

- What is happening?

- Pops, we are on the move now. No more sitting still for ages.

- Interesting. I wonder where we are going.

- In don't care, old man, we are finally moving. Could you believe it? We've made it!

- Aha, we'll see about that. I smell a rat.

- Yeah, yeah, kill joy...

In a fraction of a second, the Try Lar swayed and stopped abruptly, hitting an obstacle. The load balanced to the left and to the back, hanging awkwardly. The Wooed 'n Let's Play! Rushed towards the gates, pressing them. The gates opened, letting the Wooed 'n Let's Play! fall down the high way. All kinds of cartons of various sizes, shapes and colours spread on the street, in front of speeding trucks and vehicles of all types. It was hell. Cartonda jumped in front, where Cartongi was still sleeping, unsuspecting anything. He pushed her with one corner, yelling desperately: "Wake up, for God's sake, wake up!". Cartongi opened her eyes and started to cry.

- What is happening, what on Earth have you done now!

- It's not me this time, it is the Try Lar. I think it is an accident of some sort.

- A traffic accident, my dear, said Cartonraw.

- Who are you, Methuselah Knows-It-All?

- I understand you are angry, but it is not our fault. We are trying to help.

- Ohhh, and I was sleeping so peacefully, dreaming about arriving at my client. He was handsome and sweet, opening me with delicate moves ... My life is ruined she cried, spilling tears all over.

- Sweetie, that was a dream, the situation is different now. Put yourself together, said Cartonraw.

Cartonda got out his hands, holding Cartongi firmly, while Cartonraw seized the other hand. Their Wooed 'n Let's Play! slid to the gates.

- When I say three, we jump, said Cartonraw. Be prepared, be prepared, now! Jump!

- No, I don't want to jump, leave me alone, the system will find me!

· Sweetie, you will damage yourself falling down on the street and the system will send you to the recycling centre, where you will end up crushed by a huge metallic claw.

· No, let go of me, I don't believe you. You are liars!

· Look ahead, see the damaged carton lying broken on the street?

· Oh, this is awful...

· There is a soft grassy piece of land in this roundabout, let's jump there, we won't have big problems.

Cartonda, Cartongi Horsy and Cartonraw jumped all together, landing on that green grassy roundabout. Cartonraw slightly bumped his head, Cartongi landed on her bottom, while Cartonda fell aside, scratching his left shoulder.

· Ouch, rather painful, he whined, massaging his shoulder.

· You tell me, Cartongi replied, I can't feel my bottom anymore.

· You'll be as new in no time.

· God bless you, old man, you're a nice chap.

· Ho, ho, ho, not bad at all, ain't I?

· Pops, lead us out of it. Where are we now? asked Cartonda.

· We are on the highway, in the middle of nowhere.

· What shall we do?

· We will start walking.

· Walking? Are you crazy? Our muscles are atrophied after so much sleep.

· You will do it, trust me.

The three cartons put themselves in motion, dragging their feeble feet on the asphalt.

· My feet are killing me, said Cartongi Horsy.

· We moved exactly two metres so far.

· Oh, I won't make it, cried Cartongi.

5

- Yes, you will. We will stop now and then, aren't we, Pops?

- Hmmm, ok.

Advancing and stopping for a break at every five metres, they arrived near a deserted warehouse, finding shelter there. It just started to pour heavily, the cold rain threatening to wet their carton skin, turning them into flaccidity.

- I had enough of this. This is all your fault, Cartongi Horsy reproached Cartonda.

- Yeah, yeah, my fault every time. I know it already, save your breath for a change ...

- We'd better get inside, see what's there. It sounds better than getting soaked outside, said Cartonraw, showing them the deserted warehouse.

- Not such a bad idea, I know a guy who's a champion at this sport, said Cartongi.

The three cartons headed in the warehouse direction, where a strong, sharp metallic noise could be heard. It seemed to be an industrial machinery, fallen to the ground, creaking and echoing. The cartons stopped, scared to death, when the rain was suddenly turning into a wild storm, a real typhoon for the cardboard people. Almost tiptoeing, with his heart beating violently, Cartonda slipped through the rusty gate, inside the warehouse. Both his friends remained outside, waiting for his return, if possible. Once entered on the other side of the old fashioned metallic gate, Cartonda stopped, sharpening and straining his eyesight to grasp what's inside, ignoring his inner fear. His mind kept sending alarming or scaring thoughts, making him expect the worst. It could be a huge cardboard shredder machine, a broken, psycho chopper for recycling, escaped from scrap metal, programmed to destroy all the cartons met on its way. Cartonda heard something coming towards him. He closed his eyes, preparing to be punched.

- He is scared, boss … ha ha ha, laughed a coarse voice of a smoker.

- Yeah, yeah, he is eating worms, that's for sure … said another one, with a nasal pronunciation.

- Leave him alone, he's mine. Cutie pie, open your eyes to daddy!

Cartonda opened his eyes, finding a huge carton guy in front of him, tattooed all over his arms, neck and backside. You couldn't put a needle on his skin without piercing some vivid body artwork. His biceps were hideously pumped and his fits could crush a boulder. The boss had bald head, shining while watching Cartonda, amused, his mouth enlarged in a broad smile, without three or four teeth aside. He seemed to be an earlier series carton, produced around the fifties. Its cardboard was damaged in the front side, thin lines were cut deep into its carton pulp.

- Hi, I am Cartonda. How are you, guys?

- Not your concern. What are you doing here, Braveheart?

- I am with some friends, we are trying to take shelter, it's pouring outside.

- Ohooohoo, friends, you say?

- Yeah, I can bring them here, if you like.

- But of course, the more of them, the better, the bald headed guy grinned, hitting his knee with the right fist.

Cartonda went outside the rusty gate, all white and terrified, inviting Cartongi and Cartonraw inside.

- Look, three of them. Put them to work early in the morning. JBando, End Rew, Mere Trix, show the girl what she has to do. Bee M W Plastic ILash Woman, explain the boys what is all about, together with HellInga and Ligata. UDol Osa, Mere Trix, prepare the snake. Now, let them sleep in the corner, on that pile of dump. Everybody, it's time for sweet dreams now. All down.

5

Cartonda and his friends tried to pretend they were sleeping tight. Cartonraw was faking the snoring, Cartongi was crying soundless, tearfully, while Cartonda thought about an escape plan.

- Hey, guys, I saw a lighter in JBando's hand. I will try to sneak around and take it. We will set this place on fire, it's creepy.

Somehow, Cartonda managed to steal the lighter, it wasn't too difficult, JBando was sleeping on its belly, snoring noisily, holding an empty bottle of whisky in one hand and HellInga in the other. The lighter was near HellInga, as she tried to steal it, too. Cartonda took the lighter, set the pile of dump on fire and the three of them ran away. After a heavy drinking evening, the gang was sleeping hard. Cartonda and his friends were already outside, crossing the railway road, heading towards the town centre. Cartongi was still crying, cursing her bad luck. They heard noise behind, somebody was coming after them, firing shots.

- I will get you, bastards, wait till I lay my hands on you, the big guy was yelling in despair.

He was accompanied by two carton police officers, Cartonda saw their hats projected on the burning warehouse background. It was quite a show, the deserted warehouse was burning, the blazes reaching high.

- We are doomed, you got us into trouble again, Cartongi said. They will find us and we will be sent us back to the cardboard factory, where they will chop and dissolve us into water. We will die ....! Cartongi screamed, crying.

- Don't cry, sweety, it's bad for you complexion, Cartonraw told her.

The two police agents grabbed them, marked them as raw material and threw them into the back of a police van. They were on the way to the nearest cardboard factory now.

Hungry and tired after the chase, the agents stopped near a fast food store to buy some food.

- We could run away now, Cartonda said to his friends.
- How? Where?
- The van's door is faulty, it is not entirely closed. Take a look here.

The door was slightly opened, indeed. Cartonraw pushed it with its shoulder, opening it wider. They got out, closed back the door, running away in great speed, hiding in a trash container. Seeing a mouse within the garbage bin, Cartongi Horsy started to scream out.

- There is a mouse inside, I won't get in!
- A mouse, a single one? Is it small or big? Cartonda asked her.
- I don't know, we have to check, it could crunch our cardboard.
- Hey, pal, what are you doing here? What's your name? Cartonda enquired, a bit scared.
- I am a Nonny Mouse, the mouse replied.
- A Nonny Mouse? What is that? Cartonraw added, flabbergasted.
- A mouse that makes a living in the plastic bins, keeping low profile. Nobody bothers me here, the little mouse answered.
- Is this your home? Isn't unbreathable inside?
- It's not a home, I would say it is a hiding place, I change it quite often.
- Are you going to gnaw our cardboard? It would destroy us, you know ...
- No, I don't eat cartons when there is so much waste food, easy to get.

The three friends jumped into the bin, continuing the conversation with the Nonny Mouse, till the external sounds faded away. The agents came eating sandwiches, started the engine and drove away, without looking what's happening in the back of the van.

-What do we do now? asked Cartonraw.

-We rest here for a few hours, replied Cartonda.

-It stinks. Besides, what if they come to collect the garbage and find us here? It could be risky, Cartongi expressed her fears.

-Ok, then, let's get going.

The three cartons walked till they arrived back at the Try Lar, waiting patiently till the help came from Massy Carton Mazeotopia. A new, shiny Try Lar was loaded now with the Wooed 'n Let's Play! which collected the fallen cartons, sleeping on the street. Cartonraw and Cartongi jumped on the Wooed 'n Let's Play!, merrily.

-Come with us, don't be stupid. It's dangerous outside, on your own, Cartongi said to Cartonda.

-I am too old to face the world, Cartonraw said. I am going back on the shelves. I don't look too damaged, maybe they will not send me to recycling.

-Maybe, but I am not coming, Cartonda replied.

A lot of wrapping foil rolls quickly surrounded the cartons in a thin transparent film, inducing them a false reality. They slept without worries now, carried by the Try Lar back to Massy Carton Mazeotopia, where their fate will be decided. Cartonda disappeared into the fog, hiding behind a tree, waiting for the Try Lar to go away. "I had enough sleep, now I want to live" Cartonda told himself, smiling freely.

# THE MOUSTACHE

Primus Silicis is an ethereal presence that lives in a gigantic metallic box, dropped from the sky by a cohort of biblical angels that decided to retract from the world, for a few centuries. They packed everything they had, stacking it in an enormous plastic bag, thrown over half of the world. Possessing artificial intelligence and biological lateral extensions, this bag used to talk, reporting to the angels that the metallic case has been badly damaged, while falling. "Angel 1, report, the box is lost. Confirm location. Ready. Current status. Sleep". The assembly of cherubs considered the case's recovery would endanger their collective mission, deciding to leave it behind, check it on return. Before the most devout cherubim's disappearance, Primus Silicis used to hide himself under the floor, his approved manifestation spectre being the lowest in that spiritual environment. His ethereal composition was denser than the archangels' configuration, partly airy, partly smoggy, with bits and molecules of earthly dust and human exhalations.

In Primus Silicis, a rather impure entity, the angels could sniff the garbage on the urban streets, disposed of late at night, assorted with fermented beer and puke, damp cigarette butts and rotten meat. Disappointed, trying to avoid their presence, Primus Silicis learned how to keep himself out of sight, living suspended by the moustache underneath the floor, above the devilish gangways, on the edge of the vertical border, peopled with nocturnal powers. Purer than the demons' essence, still much less impure than the archangels' establishment, Primus Silicis infiltrated himself into the ground, letting out his black, leery, astute moustache, displayed as two sparrow wings, woven together with a wiry thread. Trying hard to act as a haphazard stain on the horizontal, inferior part of the metallic case which could, anyway, easily roll itself on every edge, depending on the solar energy intensity, Primus Silicis survived there for a few thousands of years.

One day, Primus Silicis realized that if he moved his moustache two times instead of once, he felt no vibration overhead, customarily generated by the angelic wings' flutter. For a while, he played lifting the left part of the moustache first, followed by the right one, for more than ten times. Still no vibration at the upper level, which made him think something must have been changed. Inquisitive and alerted, Primus Silicis flung himself above, balancing his feet up and down, circling the thin line that separated what's up from what's down, till he gained depth in the upper region of the massive box. Happy that he eventually moved in the opposite, but the right direction, Primus Silicis materialized a toy train assembled on the ceiling, as he got accustomed to always see things overhead, for so many millennia. Another way to have fun by himself was to stand on his hands, watching his own moustache's reflection in the acrylic rubber underlay floor, when the gigantic box wasn't turning upside down by itself. This way, he could observe it thoroughly, from every perspective, until he got bored, reducing his presence to an imperceptible line on one of the colossal, steel cage's flawed panels.

# METALAND

Somewhere, there is an intriguing world, inhabited by enchanted beings that walk right on the blue, luminous sky, functioning as a virtual and concrete floor, try to imagine. These mysterious beings are very tall and possess shiny, metallic bodies, made out of gold, brass, copper, silver and other glittery metals. Whenever the Metalanders feel emotion, the metal liquefies, springing up gently, flowing down like a mountain wellhead, vibrating and purling in a glossy bright whirl, as if the sunshine is pouring on them. I was about to enter their world, when a sequence of unfortunate events pressed me back into the ordinary, after spinning around in a roundabout, suddenly changing direction, turning on the opposite course of the road.

If you want to reach this world, follow my instructions cautiously, completely *mot-a-mot*. Watch out not to brake your front door key in two halves while turning it inside the lock, right before driving to work. Be careful, don't allow any dog to wag its tail when passing by you. Be attentive to any van delivering groceries to a neighbour on your street, while a special song is played on TV, at the exact moment when your partner is going outside to check on his car, as if unintended. Be alert, notice the other car immediately driving on the street, read its number plate and write it down, if possible. Try to remember, earlier, the evening before yesterday, your partner mimicked lame walk while entering a supermarket with a particular add exposed at the entrance, where he was supposed to buy a specific product. I know he likes custard, he secretly dreams about swimming in an ocean of creamy, sweet vanilla custard, canned, ready-made, home-maid, ordered online, served chilled or hot, with whipped cream and fruit, ignoring the fact that he could sink in, fall on the bottom, drag you down there with him.

Mind the gap, the flew jab, the cooking recipe of the day, the advice to double your meal, the diet based on fat. Be vigilant when acquiring brown or cane sugar, be watchful to fill in the bottle correctly, be extremely careful when humming your favourite song, while he winks the right or left eye, when choosing the bus, when clicking the desired entertainment menu bar on Internet. Be alert when he fills in the form at the surgery, when you join a recruiting agency, when you start induction, when you navigate online, when you follow or you are followed by fans on social media, when you or him take part in a tombola to win a new bin or a shed for your house. Stop buying lots of mayonnaise, it's not healthy, think before donating old belongings to charity, and, especially, when you take out the waste bin for recycling. Be cautious and better not try to walk alone on the street after 11 pm, especially if you are a woman, you could be followed by a drunkard approaching from behind, out of nowhere.

If you avoided all the inappropriate steps, you would notice that the whole street would dance with you, a complete flash-mob. This rocket was already launched, begin to prepare for the next one, and please don't forget any detail, no matter how insignificant it might seem. *oo oo 22 11 CDR Roger. There's nothing like an interesting launch. oo oo 22 14 CC That's right. Oo oo 23 14 CC Apollo 13, Houston. Canary LOS in 30 seconds. Request COMMAND RESET, please.*

# THE POOL

She was walking aimlessly in the boiling sun, feeling she could evaporate in the fiery sun, as if burned at stake. Suddenly, she found herself naked, in a black plastic bag, thrown away in the desert. At first, Julie thought she is dead, but she was still alive, numb and woozy, with a terrible headache. When touching her hair with the left hand, massaging it, she discovered coagulated blood, mixed with igneous black plastic bag, on the top of her head. The woman started to walk on the hot sand, staggering, when she thought she caught glimpse of a pool in front of her. The water pool materialized and disappeared, out of nowhere, exasperating her, now it was here and in the next moment it was gone.

Julie couldn't remember who she was, what her name was, and what had happened to her, how she ended up in the desert. *But being heated by the Sun on his journey, he bent his bow at the god, who in admiration of his hardihood, gave him a golden gablet in which he crossed the ocean.* A fantastic animal appeared near her, out of the blue, made of ice, able to walk and wag its furry tail, without melting in the desert sun. The woman wasn't amazed, she took the animal in her arms, to cool off, petting it, whispering "Don't worry, don't cry, everything is going to be all right, you'll see". The small pet smiled at her, and climbed on the top of her head, just like a monkey, shading and cooling her fevered cranium. She collapsed, lifeless, while the animal licked her face, the icy sensation bringing her back to reality.

All at once, Julie noticed a dark vertical whirl, connecting the sky with the sands, pouring dark matter on the ground.

Distant whispers, hissings and a tune could be heard, somebody was singing a song in an unknown language. She narrowed her eyes to take a better look, but the sun was blinding her. When the woman looked down, she noticed the pool was there again, dense and murky, tempting her to dive inside. First, she touched it with her toes, it seemed to be viscous, pitch like, as the black liquefied plastic bag, yet it was cold and refreshing as a summer rain in August.

The woman plunged into that creamy liquid, her skin, reddened by the terrible, ruthless sun, got impregnated with the dark plasma. The dark matter penetrated her epidermis strata, infiltrating deep inside her body, into the internal organs and cells, modifying her DNA. She was absorbed by the pool, dissolved within. A murmur could be heard, together with a subtle vibration and the cosmic plasma pool repositioned itself as an alien space ship, preparing to take off. "Thank you for your kind offering", an enigmatic voice uttered, "Now we have enough energy to travel to another planet". The ship disappeared, and nobody was there to witness the extraordinary occurrence.

# THE LUGGAGE

Gary entered the airport to check in the baggage, a huge, black, plastic luggage bought from Germany years ago. He was about to miss his plane, at least that's what he assumed, and as his holiday was over, he was expected to go back to the warehouse where he was working with colleagues from all over the world. Inside his hometown airport, crowds of people waited in line, running in all directions, in great urgency. First, Gary headed towards the check-in desk where three young women stood, then hurried to another counter, when suddenly disappeared. She saw it clearly, a giant dragon flew on the ceiling, spitting fire on the black luggage, the three women laughed, turning very old for a few seconds, as if somebody was forwarding a movie very fast. Right that moment, the baggage opened, letting the clothes fly away, rising above the heads.

It was not windy inside, just a bit of air conditioned, although it couldn't explain why his costumes were, beguilingly, taken up, while he was there, in every suite, looking younger or older, sadder or happier, smiling or frowning, surprised or over confident, the way he might have been when he wore them. She saw him up there, floating, multiplied in an endless series of life stages lived together, more or less. Then, he disappeared completely. No trace of him, since then. His wife reported him missing, however the authorities couldn't find him. They asked the wife to write a report on the unusual event, where she richly described the dragon's appearance, the three girls turning into hags, the black luggage opening wide and the suits, costumes and clothes containing him in various lifetime moments, floating above.

The authorities questioned a series of people about the unusual happening, it seemed that nobody had seen anything. An old man from a distant mountain village thought he saw the missing man boarding the plane together with a tanned, dark-haired woman, whose strands of hair seemed to be waving as long, thin, black snakes, hissing. A woman wearing thick, square glasses noticed a man resembling him, accompanied by a dark haired woman, arriving in London airport. They dragged a black, plastic baggage after them, which seemed heavier and heavier as they neared the airport exit door. Out of the airport, the baggage remained stuck on the pavement, barking with a toothed grin. People around got scared, the luggage couldn't be moved anymore, and the missing man and the woman left it there, quickly getting on the bus.

That is all they could find out about him. She has never seen him again, and since then, she keeps dreaming about him getting lost into a black luggage, arranged as any other exit door, heading to a dark, mysterious and scary tunnel, where the three young women were waving to him. They were the three Parcae, waving his life thread, ripping it into small pieces, after he passed by them. Once inside, he fell down to the ground, motionless, numb, almost dead. Every time, she tried to pull him out of the dark corridor, where he was lying down, stunned, but he was heavy as a mountain. The dragon came close, flying, changing into a dark-haired woman, when touching ground. She put her hand above him and he stood up, following her, blindly, towards a crowd of demons and monsters, shadows and animals, sinking into a pile of dirt and altered waste.

# DEPOSITUM CUSTODI

*He come on moonlight rays as elemental dust*

Depositum Custodi seemed an ordinary warehouse, dusty, stuffy and cold, populated with rusty metallic shelves. Moris started working there for a couple of days only, when he realized strange entities meander inside. One early morning, he was driving the vehicle on the 55 aisle, when he thought he saw a sparkle dancing in the air. It was only a second, but he managed to notice it, even though he didn't give it too much attention. After all, he hasn't slept too well the previous nights, it could have been an optical illusion. Next day, he was passing on the same aisle, and the spark danced around him for half a second. Moris felt a subtle vibration around his head, tending to reverberate around his body. Next day, nothing happened. After two more days, the spark materialized again, coming down towards him, suddenly penetrating his head. The man felt a pinching sensation, something like a light electrocution, shaking him brutally. He got dizzy, the eyelids became heavy as the lead and almost lost his balance.

He stopped the headset and went to the toilet, to wash his face, trying to refresh his mind. Heading towards the bathroom, while turning left, he saw a door frame vibrating in the air, inviting him to pass through. The man walked that way, almost hypnotized, hearing whispered commands in his mind. "Walk three steps. Stop. Turn around. Close your eyes. Stop. Walk two steps. Stop. Open your eyes". When he opened the eyes, he had a terrible fright, realizing he was floating in the air, above a dark, endless void, shaped as a cone, very sharp on the bottom. Its bottom was a point in space, the tip of a very sharp needle. "Don't blink, don't move a muscle, or you'll fall down in the abyss and never come back". "What's down there?" he uttered in his mind. "This is the chronological depth of the temporal dimension of the Universe".

He felt a vibration in the stomach and a slight circular movement. Second by second, Moris was whirling in the null space, as the Vitruvian Man round his own axe, at the same time leaning perfectly horizontally, suspended on an invisible energy chord, while the chronological void was slowly turning upside down, aiming its sharp tip towards his head, right between the eyes, rotating fast. The movement opened his head and the brain, at the same time, turning it into light. The luminous matter extended till comprised all his body, causing a small explosion. He was now a collection of star dust, floating in the Universe, capable to cross it, instantly, from one end to the other. *As for the Light that existed before the world, the intellectual and essential wisdom that was before time itself...*

# THE PARKING LOT

The car turned left to the downtown parking lot, near the church built in the 19th century, stopping in front of the church gate, letting noisy music out to pierce the silence and heavy smoke of cigarettes to poison the air. TJ opened the car door and put one foot on the concrete, while the asphalt bent down, rocking the car aside, on two wheels. It was in the middle of a sunny day, at the end of August, when, all of a sudden, the daylight went dim and milky, hanging low on the pavement, covering the church building into a thick fog. TJ returned at the driving wheel, running the car in reverse, trying to leave the parking zone, when an ice storm hurled over the city, the hazy light being sectioned by thunders and lightnings. In the next moment, a giant monster carrying immense lead hammers instead of hands has arisen from the Earth, drumming the car.

Terrified, the driver tried to continue running the car backwards, when the grass round about behind him turned into a huge mouth with the tongue out and appalling, bulky fangs. The monster roared and tonnes of fresh blood poured over the parking, rising above the other vehicles, together with chopped human and animal body parts. *And so upon you will come all the righteous blood shed on earth.* The driver started to scream in horror, striving to figure out what to do to escape, to find refuge in a peaceful place, where the sky can be blue, the daylight clear and the raindrops clean. *He makes me lie down in green pastures, /he leads me beside quiet waters, /He refreshes my soul.*

A lightning set the sky on fire, afterwards a strong light hit the parking, blinding the driver. He raised his hands to cover the eyes, when he woke up in his car, in the parking lot, where he was sleeping in the dense, stinky cigarette smoke, drunk after a night long concert. Dizzy and scared, he drove to his parents, who lived on the nearby street. TJ really felt the need to take a shower, eat a fresh home-made vegetable soup, and read literature. *At every moment there was one more of those innumerable and humble 'selves' that compose our personality ...*

# MEMORIES

*Then I hope his ghost will haunt you*

It was a living nightmare, she was thrown out of her own house, by her own family. Andrea's memories deserted her, leaving behind a horrible certitude, her husband parted with her for another woman. The wife and mother lives in an asylum now, where strange people guard her. Andrea is a patient. Her mind ceded, forgetting who she is or has ever been, with mixed come back episodes, convincing the family that her place is somewhere else, where she would be well taken care of by specialists. Now and then, she wakes up, realizing bits and shreds of reality, broken memories of her former life. When her husband came to visit her with their daughters, she asked the youngest one who is that woman her husband had the nerve to come there to visit her. It was outrageous to expose themselves there, humiliating her. Andrea would never agree on that. But it seems it was the first daughter, who takes the most after her. Then she forgot to drink water for a week, or maybe she thought there is no reason to do that anymore.

The woman almost died. She does not know yet, maybe will never understand or will never be able to retain the truth: her husband is not here anymore, he disappeared into the unknown, passing towards the final mystery. One day later, she had a riot with another patient, for an unknown reason. The other woman claimed she had a dialogue with her husband the night before. They talked a lot about several things, even about her. "No, I don't believe you" said the wife, crying. "It's true, though, he was here, with me, in my room" the other replied. They fought desperately, hating each other awfully.

For the next days, Andrea remained in her room, alone, refusing to get out, waiting for her husband to come and see her. She was trying hard to stay awake all night long. One night, she couldn't sleep at all, even after taking sleep aid pills. She felt terribly irritated, going to the bathroom multiple times. In the middle of the night, he came. First, it was a foggy micro-galaxy of lights, flying quickly above her bed, horizontally, where she was lying down. Star dust, golden flickers of energy. Fiery pixels. Luminous, glittering dots, gathered together in an irregular, yet homogeneous shape. She felt surprised by the ethereal presence passing above her, slightly sketched, a microscopic replica of the Milky Way, whirling right above her body, in great speed. An unfinished image in a child's naïve drawing.

"Is it you?" she asked, in her mind. "It is me", came the answer, as a waft on her cheeks. When the carers opened the door to her room next morning, she was gone. They found a blurred picture of the married couple, in their twenties, holding hands, lying carelessly on the floor. Turning it on the other side, another image could be seen, this time a picture of them together, older. When hold against the window light, they moved slowly, as in a slow motion movie projected from a different dimension. In the next moment, it burst into fire, turning into a small particles of ash, scattered in the air.

# THE SLEEPWALKING

*She was bitten by the vampire when she was in a trance, sleep-walking*

One night, Judie Harriet was walking down the country road, heading to the next hamlet. The woman was wearing a white robe, brightened by the moon light. Although her eyes were closed, she was stepping regularly on the middle, endless line, separating the two opposite directions. In the darkness, a foggy, whitish shape loomed out, bouncing from one hill to another. No houses around, no cars rolling, not even a village cart, just the limitless road, going forth, undulating in the distance, like a huge, concrete dragon snake. The misty, asymmetrical shape neared and faded away, leaping on the knolls, in the four corners. She felt currents of air on her face, easily fluttering strings of hair, blowing them on her complexion. Then, or maybe at the same time, she wasn't sure about it, came a whisper, echoing in the wide, barren space. A swing was rocking and the misty creature was on it, singing a children's song, reverberated around. In the next moment, she was swaying on the white swing, which lifted her high above, rocking over the top of the hills, up to the sky and back. "What if I fell down", it crossed her mind.

Still, she went on, singing and rocking, singing and rocking, swaying in the air, above the hills, reaching the sky, as if she was in a broken plane, flying back and forth, up and down, constantly. Judie Harriet was walking again on the road, in the darkness, then swaying, till she got frightened and screamed. She found herself in bed, wet with perspiration and tear drops. She couldn't see around. "Am I blind?" she wondered, feeling her face with the hands. The face and the eyes were swollen, something warm flew down her dress, reddening it. "Is it blood, my blood?". She screamed strongly and woke up again, in her bed, sleeping. "What a nightmare!" she said, turning on a small lamp to swallow a calming pill. The woman tried to find the explanation for the nightmare's cause, it could be a distress caused by diffuse thoughts, ruminated late at night, when the shadows replace the lights, darkening delicate foreheads. This is the time when anything seems murkier, ghostly phantasms roaming in the corners of the mind, quickly shattered by the dawns. Or it could be the old house, built hundreds of years ago, inhabited by the reminiscences and recalls of the former owners, hiding inside, till the end of time.

# THE SYRINGE

*CDR I believe we've had a problem here*

Discontented with its fate, a single use, dispensable object, the syringe lost its patience. Realizing that, the Easy Touch safety syringe found itself trapped into a sterile, mean, claustrophobic foil, closed inside a transparent plastic box. All the other syringes, be it with or without needles, oral or otherwise, were having forty winks, totally unaware of the current situation. Given that she couldn't elude the concrete conditions, the syringe withdrew into its own imagination. Lying there, horizontally, day and night, without being able to move a single millimetre, the syringe started to think it might be an Apollo 13 Boeing rocket, with a Lunar Module Adaptor, a Third Stage S-IVB, a Second Stage S-II, a First Stage S -IC, two J 2 engines, a Lunar Roving Vehicle, together with Command and Service Modules. Unfortunately, the Launch Escape System was missing.

Soon, the syringe got bored to be a rocket, without having the slightest chance of exploring the deep cosmic space. It's not fun at all to be a ground missile, it is even worse than being a common hypodermic. Such a grand destiny! The whole Universe as a playground! So many possibilities ahead, and absolutely no means to fructify them ... *A series of three dots (...) is used to designate those portions of the text that could not be transcribed because of garbling.* At that point, a new idea sparkled inside its mind: to turn into a fish. A streamlined,

7

slippery fish, which can swim horizontally and vertically, well-thought the injection-some of them can even jump out of the water, like the mountain trout. Indeed, a full bouquet of aquatic, ichthyologic potentials and prospects.

The heart leapt in the syringe's chest, and stopped immediately. A fish is bound to live in the water, it could die if dares to desert its environment! This could be a factual problem, an unmanageable obstacle, without a doubt. What else could it be? Oh, yes, it could be a proudly designed, full flex, superfine carbon cork for fishing rods, meant to catch the fish. Throw the bait, wait and elegantly extract the fish from its atmosphere, for instance a river, a lake or a small stream pocket water, expose it to oxygen and see what happens.

# MORTA

Morta was an Agaricus bisporus Champignon mushroom accidentally grown into the forest, in the first taciturn weeks of the spring. Over the winter, she was a small seed in the ground, pulsating regularly in a vigorous rhythm, trying to break through the multiple strata of fat land. Morta was so small, lost down there in the darkness, a blind, vegetal, soft shred, striving to cross the layers of the loose earth, to see the light. In the subterraneous zone, there was no sunlight, nor was enough air to breath, and even the rain water was occasional. Suffocated, she counted to three, retracted within herself, then sprang up, blindfoldedly, through the thick strata of brown dirt. She was very scared, at first thinking she would die, in the next moment fearing she would fall down, even lower than before. She tried to feel her big head and the round, short, stumpy body, to check if everything was in its normal position, sighing in relief. She wasn't upside down, but a bit oriented to the left upper side. In a few seconds, it seemed as if Morta was going round like a wheel, in complete circles, causing her dizziness. Her brains started to boil.

Morta closed her eyes, trying to calm down, focus on her long term objective – to reach the sky. Being so brave, ambitious and unquestionably white, the Portobello mushroom considered she deserves the best that can be found in the world, beneath and above. Squeezed inside, as she grew, Morta needed wider space, more resources - water, air, and sunshine. She stretched her big, patchy, round head, pushed

7

her stalky body forward, into the deadly nightshade, forcing the earth to move a millimetre. It took a lot of effort and energy to make that exhausting toil, determining Morta to instantly fell asleep. She napped three days in a row, dreaming ambiguous dreams about herself trying to push away a mountain, striving to make her way up in the daylight. Morta sweltered heavily, the sweat drops burning her skin, dripping down the meaty stalk, softening the unyielding land.

She couldn't move and her back remained curbed in an uncomfortable position. The bisporus mushroom stood there for a while, it really felt like centuries, crying and screaming for help. When she finally woke up, she was still there, the earth moved a millimetre, and that was, truthfully, a success. The Portobello mushroom prepared to heave up, encouraged by the last accomplishment, heartened by the fact that it is possible to move little by little, even if it is only a ludicrous distance of a millimetre. After all, Morta was just a shoot of a mushroom, a mere possibility of a vegetal existence, almost an illusion. She was still invisible, trapped into the ruthless, merciless, dark ground, where one had to fight to rise above and let the world know about her existence. Imagining herself up into the daylight, enthusiasm and energy filled her like a cup, helping her sprout other two millimetres. Morta was bigger now, didn't feel too weary for that matter, and she thought it wiser to rest a bit, to recover her strength.

Before falling asleep, she carefully made plans and strategies for her long term objectives, calculating her body surface and weight, deployed in the earthly vastness. "This land, it must be enormous", she assumed. "I really must get up there and see it with my own eyes". In that particular moment, she felt wings growing on her back, lifting her up a few centimetres, allowing her to boost her head up, above the surface. She screamed out of joy, the entire body being transformed into an arch, propelling her above. Morta was able to see bits of the surface now. Out of joy, she jumped on her stalk once or twice, lifting the head to see more of it. It was early morning, the sky was clear and bluish, the morning star and the crescent still sparkled, gradually losing luminosity. The mushroom saw little leaves of grass trying to shoot above, yet it was her who was gushing up first. It was a pinching cold, during a foggy and metallic morning, at the break of spring, when all the plants and animals want to come back to life, kicking, hitting and fighting in their blind will to be.

And Morta was already there to see it, feel it and tell others the tale of the unflinching, stupidly stubborn life, ridiculously and completely unimaginative. Disappointed, she thought about going back downwards again, in that thick darkness, where her onward movement was possible, where she was able to defeat the vast, earthen enormity that enveloped her in a tight, profound hug.

# THE NOBLE GREEN HORSE

One late night, I thought I fell asleep, but actually, as it seems, I didn't, because odd events started to take place. A huge spider's shadow crawled on the window, giving chills down my spine, while the TV screen whirled and became a black hole, spitting out a fauna of the strangest creatures. A white dinosaur wearing high heels jumped for joy, laughing out loud. It was a lady, looking for her match, telling me that she had to wait 50.000 years for the ritual, compliant with their pre-historic rites. Unfortunately, she dropped dead in the next second, cardiac arrest, her body turning into dust on a pile of bones. A grey, old turtle creeped down really slowly, circling around its back shell, which suddenly opened to show an ancient library. Regrettably, the old parchments, scrolls and manuscripts were eaten by mice, insects and parasites, half of them being wet and musty.

Strange, incomplete characters, places and inkhorn situations kept getting out of the books, floating above: Hercules performing his twelfth labour, a few columns of an ancient temple, an emperor's head, Cleopatra's nose, Adam's rib, Achilles' ankle, a rotten quarter of the wooden Trojan Horse, Venus of Milo's hands, Hamlet's skull, king Lear's beard etc. The shell closed back, hiding all the unpredicted agitation of its written, illusionary population. A brown bird flew above, hitting against the walls, spinning around the chandelier, cawing. An arrow hit her, it fell down, and a haruspex cut its abdomen, to read the omens in its internal organs. A lightning stroke. The flash faded away, when I noticed a green horse coughed, sitting down on a pink armchair, his legs crossed. He wore a blue, long coat, with a sparkling, foamy, white collar, yellow stockings and black shoes. He blinked regularly, studying me in great amazement, trying not to show its emotion, according to the etiquette.

- What are you doing in my room? he asked, quite astonished.

- I, I, I, aaaahhhaaaa, this is my room, actually, I live here for many months now, I replied, stuttering, a bit shocked.

- I don't recall leaving the house or selling it. Are you a jester of the court? the horse replied embarrassed, twisting his belt.

- No, I am not a jester.

- Then are you a lunatic from the hospital?

- No, why are you asking that?

- You look strange, your clothes are weird. I have never seen something like that.

- Neither have I ever seen a talking horse before.

- I am a special horse, an educated one, a true gentleman.

The horse coughed again, clearing his voice and added:

- Sorry, I have not introduced myself. My name is Scribo, I am a thoroughbred horse, a count and a renowned poet, he said, standing up, bowing down to me.

- What poems do you write?

- Sonnets, usually. Very elaborated, rhymed and locked, like a code.

- Love sonnets?

- They seem so, I start from a simple emotion, a mere illusion, and construct a text which flows, soft, in my hands, like a stream of water. I turn it into ice, I mould it, then I let it melt again.

- What is the code?

- I don't know, I always ask myself what is the process of casting my thoughts and feelings into words. It seems magical, actually. But I feel it is more than that, and the final product is more complex than a string of melodic words. A combination. A memory storing, traces of a life. Shadow theatre, signs on a paper boulevard. Temporary and vulnerable, as beauty, as life.

- That is truly amazing, I said. I am writing, too.

- What do you write? Scribo asked.

- I write short stories.

- What is that, short stories?

- Patches of histories, biographies, actions or events. Individual, collective, cosmic.

- Interesting, and strange, too. Why not long stories?

- Good question. Some of them are not short, actually. It depends on how much time I have on my hands.

- Mine are classic poems, very rhymed, almost mechanically. I wish I could write in a more extravagant way, like a mad man or something ....

- Plunge into your mind, dig deeper.

- I can't escape reality, it has a grip on me. Won't let go, it holds me really tight.

- Try to release yourself of its girths. Close your eyes and imagine you are a flower.

- I can't be a flower ... it is so small, delicate, perfumed and, and vulnerable ...

- Think, it can be a carnivorous flower. That one is dangerous.

- Yes, in an isolated jungle. There is no escape, beasts lurking everywhere.

- Horrible monsters in the surroundings, eager to eat you, and the enchanting flower you are admiring is preparing to consume you, splashing poisonous fluids on your skin.

The green horse was so outraged by the idea that his colour started to shift from green to vernil, fluctuating to a light azure with greenish whirls. The hues tremored, vanishing gradually, and this is how I got rid of that naughty, surreal animal, which had the nerve to consider itself such a remarkable, agreeable, talented, noble gentleman.

# A FISH IN MY YELLOW CUP

A few years ago, after a long and agitated night, I woke up early in the morning, almost crawling downstairs, eyes practically closed. When I arrived in the kitchen, I heard a stifled noise, drowned in water. Surprised, I looked that way, noticing something moving in my yellow tea jug. It was a grey fish, with purple spots on its back, swimming relaxed in the cup, enjoying the summer weather. It was the end of August, when the sunshine warms the roof and the walls of the house, turning it into a sauna, the best way to cool yourself being to take a shower or plunge into a swimming pool. Thinking it is a dream or some kind of hallucination, I pinched my arm. The fish was still there, having its fun in the yellow jug.

· Hey, this is my cup. What are you doing here? I asked the intruder, annoyed by the view.

· No, this is mine. I am here for a long time, the odd fish replied.

· I have never seen you before, that's for sure.

· Your problem, not mine.

· What do you mean, "your problem"?

· I am entitled to swim, peacefully, in this cup.

· No, you are not.

· You are rude. I can eat you, if you are edible. What species are you?

· I won't tell you.

- Tell me, then, who gave you the permission to enter my cup?

- My adviser.

- Where is he or it?

- It is a blue whale, in the Atlantic.

- Can you communicate with it? I need to ask it a few questions. I consider this a breaking in.

- You are exaggerating it. The idea is that, usually, I make myself invisible. This is the first time you are able to see me.

- This is a bunch of lies. Invisible, you say? And I drink my water, tea or juice with you inside?

- Yes.

- Don't you get burned by the hot tea?

- No, not at all, if I am invisible. When I see you approaching with the boiling water, I quickly jump into the sink.

- I don't believe you. You are an illusion, a hallucination, a product of my imagination.

- If it helps you, then I am.

- How come that you can speak?

- I come from a different world, where animals, plants and objects can talk, too.

- Where is this land?

- It is not a land, it is a dimension parallel to your reality, bordering it.

- So you say that in your world animals, plants and even objects talk?

- Yes.

- With sounds, moving their lips?

- The sounds or the physical outline is not really necessary, actually.

- Then you are all invisible?

- Something like that, we have to protect ourselves.

Otherwise, people could destroy us. Like you want to do it, now.

- I don't want to destroy you ...

- Yes, you thought I was breaking in.

- I am sorry, but it's true. You are intruding.

- I am an intruder, you say.

- Yes. Let me understand it, thoroughly. We, humans, share our houses with secret, invisible species of animals, plants and objects who are able to think and talk.

- Yes.

- This sounds horrible. I thought this is my space, my intimacy. Your place is not here. You have to go.

- Here I am. If you are offended by my presence, I will leave.

- Never come back here again. Tell all your friends I am not tolerating your presence! I screamed, trying hard to deliver my message to all its kind.

With a splash, the fish enlarged itself, growing as big as a whale, then disappeared completely. Since that day, I keep hearing subtle noises around me, especially at night, when the sleep keeps away. Sometimes, I can see giraffes, elephants and leopards playing in my courtyard; extremely perfumed flowers in the bedroom, all kind of strange vegetables in the kitchen. One day, I found a piglet in the fridge, trying to cool itself. A hyena was hiding in the oven, one late night. This uncontrollable chaos made me decide it is high time to move away, try to find a proper, normal, intimate house to live in.

# SCIURIDAE

Jada was a young Rodentia, drifting with her Sciuridae family from Eastern Europe to a foreign country. Her father, a Spermophilus Citellus remained in his old, native country, with a new, younger chipmunk and their unofficial cub. Jada and what was left of her family had a dangerous journey, facing horrible weather, strong winds, directionless cars and other vehicles. They thought about hiding in a private aeroplane and travel faster, safer than any squirrel could ever think of, hiding under the baggage. When they finally entered the air space of the new country, a customs officer welcomed them, blowing a red plastic whistle. He checked their papers, scrutinizing Jada for a second longer than the rest of the scurry. Arriving at their new nest, Jada slept for two days, but when she woke up, she was delighted to crunch some delicious nuts.

Jada took her lunch box, heading for school, where she could meet new friends, learn and have some fun. The Rodent Educational Institution was a charity large wooden house, situated in the backyard of a multi-storeyed building. For a whole academic year, Jada wasn't able to understand what the teaching team was saying or doing. Slowly, she started to understand a word here and there, then two, then four. Eating the new food, Jada grew into a fine squirrel, with greyish fur, a brown, round, finely curbed nose, two cute ears and a bushy tail. All more or less eligible alpha chipmunks started to parade in front of her, trying hard to impress in a preposterous dance mating ritual. They held their tails up, bouncing back and forth, apparently searching for something in the grass, while chasing each other. First, Jada was amazed, bursting into a childish laughter, without understanding anything. Gradually, she realized the males are trying to communicate something, still surreptitious, ambiguous, furtive to her.

Soon, she learned to act the same way, sipping water with her head up, laughing noisily, attracting everybody's attention. She enjoyed it, noticing that males are sensitive to her conduct. Jada started smoking, enjoying to act as a grown-up, even though not all of them have this habit. The squirrel began to experience stomach aches and several unknown health problems. More than that, she felt a terrible home-sickness, missing her boy-friend she would have liked to stay with, but she had to return to the foreign country. She still dreams about going back to her country, relatives and friends, like a great part of the Chordata Vertebrata Mammalia Rodentia, actually, but they are nurturing the idea in reticent silence and sapient patience.

# JASON

Jason is a well-behaved boy that goes to school every day, except for holidays, when he stays in bed for a few hours more, in the morning. He dreams about treacherous adventures in a far-away land, fighting with dangerous pirates and terrible monsters, rescuing beautiful princesses or recovering lost bounties. When he gets off his bed, he comes down into the living room, grabbing the phone in one hand and the tablet in the other, choosing what game to play: ancient battles, modern wars, incredibly valuable bounties, hideous monsters. He plays on and on, feeling no hunger nor thirst, till he gets dizzy. That day, the boy reached for a bar of chocolate washed with a can of juice, consumed while playing. In a few minutes, he felt a nasty stomach ache.

His mom texted, telling him the food is in the kitchen, on a tray. She worked as clerk at a supermarket chain, his parents living separately, lately. In fact, they were never married. Since his father left to Yolks, to live with another woman, Lana, Jason felt deserted and thrown to the garbage bin. He never talked about it, even if his friend, Rick, keeps asking. Jason found himself helplessly stuck in a hostage situation, without the power to influence his parents, to retain his father. He was sad, irritated, sometimes aggressive. First, he thought it was his mother's fault, but then realized it was the other woman's doing. He slowly fell down within himself as in an abyss, trapped inside, screaming from deep down there, trying to get out. Nobody heard him or nobody

9

cared. Now, the situation seems to worsen, his mom has a new partner, who is supposed to come and live with them, soon. Pillian, the man, has a child from a previous relationship, an annoying boy named Castys.

Irritated, he sighed and walked to the kitchen, took the tray without looking what's on it and returned. Jason stepped wrongly, losing a slipper. He hobbled, wearing only one slipper, carrying the tray unbalanced, dropping some milk on the way. Trying to hold the tray, the boy stumbled over the missed slipper and fell down, hitting his head on the floor. For a few minutes, the boy remained there, lying unconsciously, waking up when his t-shirt got soaked in milk. Bizarrely, Jason felt he is raising to the ceiling, falling back immediately. Amazed, the boy did it again, feeling light as a feather, taken by the wind, flying higher above the tallest tree on the street, after passing through the window glass, without breaking it. "This is fun", Jason thought, exultant. He did not feel hunger, thirst or pain, not even the sensation of the body weight, nor the gravitational force. Oddly, he was as light as a feather. The boy tried to feel his body, but the limbs seemed to have no consistency.

"What is happening to me?" asked himself, confused and terrified, rising again to look for his mother. "She is the only one who can help me, I got to find her". Jason arrived at her work place, entered the office and stood in front of his mom, she seemed to be in a meeting. Jason told her that he thinks something is wrong, he cannot feel his body. Surprisingly, his mother did not pay any attention to him, as if he was invisible. "Mom, why are you not listening to me? I am so scared!" Jason cried. Without responding to him, the woman stood up straightaway, telling her colleagues that she must make an urgent phone call, being worried that something wrong could have happened home. There was no answer, so she decided to go straight home, calling the emergency in the car, telling them she suspects something happened with her son, home alone, while she was at work.

When she parked in front of the house, she saw the entrance door broken. The woman rushed inside, finding Jason on the floor, being resuscitated by the emergency team. "Oh my god, Jason!" she cried. "We have pulse", the doctor said. "He is saved". They took him to the hospital, where he stayed for a few days, with a TV, his mother's tablet and his personal mobile phone. One day, playing Stormfall, he accidentally touched the remote, turning on the TV. He did not lift his eyes to watch, didn't mind the volume, till he heard noises of a battle, yells and somebody calling out "Jason". He looked up and saw a man dressed in a very unusual costume, fighting an appalling monster.

Suddenly attentive, Jason watched the fight, at the same time searching the legend of Jason and the Golden Fleece on his tablet. Jason was the son of Aeson, ruler of Iolcus, educated by Chiron the Centaurus. One day, Pelias, Aeson's step-brother, takes over the kingdom by force. Years passed, Jason grew up into a fine young man who comes back, claiming the right to the kingdom, fulfilling the prophecy of the feared appearance of a one shoed man. The condition to regain the rights is a risky expedition to the faraway lands, in search for the Golden Fleece. Since Pelias, his father's step-brother, has taken the kingdom, Jason lived in the mountains, being minded and educated by Chiron the Centaurus. Navigating online, Jason found a digital book, plus a lot of animated websites about the Golden Fleece, among them *Argonautica*, where he read about the sacrifice on a distant land.

The Argonauts were making offerings to god Apollo, slaughtering a young bull: *Come then and receive this sacrifice at our hands, far-darting god; which we have set before thee; a first gift, as an offering for our embarking on this ship.* Then they chopped the sacred thighs and burnt them, poured libations and interpreted the will of the god in the flames and smoke. Jason embarked on the ship named Argo with a crew of fifty fearful heroes, all of them in search for the Golden Fleece in mysterious kingdoms. "So that's why they were called the Argonauts!", he realized, reading. What about this Golden Fleece, Jason has never heard of a sheep endowed with Golden Fleece, it is all simple, ordinary, sometimes dirty wool.

Finally, he found data about it, there was once a Golden Fleeced Ram who manages to save two children, named Phrixus and Helle, from certain death, orchestrated by their step-mother, Ino. The children are finally saved by the Ram with the Golden Fleece, a Hermes' gift for their mother, Nephele. The Golden Fleeced Ram kidnapped the children, flying with them to Colchis; later on, Phrixus, the boy, will kill the Ram, to steal its golden fleece. The children's real father will kill his own son and Ino's, Learchus. Heartbroken, Ino throws herself into the sea together with her daughter, Melicertes, becoming marine divinities. Athamas, their father, meanders all over the world, finally settling in Thessalia, Athamantia. Jason has fallen asleep, leaving the TV play by itself, pour all the characters in the hospital room, with the din of battle and rattling weapons.

# MR. BITTERN

Mr. Bittern lives on Knockerdown Street, in Hounslow, a small town in Britain. He is a sixty five years old clerk, who worked for forty years at the county council, managing recycling, rubbish and waste department. He wakes up every morning at 6 o'clock sharp, shuffling his feet to the bathroom, where he thoroughly washes his hands, face and teeth. Afterwards, he wipes his face with a rugged cotton towel, once white, now of an unidentifiable colour, leaving it red as a tomato. The old man comes downstairs clinging to the handrail with both hands, stepping aside on the narrow stairs, gasping, mumbling coarse words. Arriving downstairs, he catches his breath, straightening his back, sweating. "We were lucky today, no falling down, Angela, my dear".

Humming a Rolling Stone's song, he prepares his breakfast, toast and butter, eggs and bacon, sips a cup of hot tea with milk, listening to the radio. Finishing the meal, Mr. Bittern grabs an old brown briefcase and steps out on the street, exactly at 7.45. Mr. Bittern walks slowly, hobbling, struggling to breathe, sweltering heavily, wearing his faded beige rain coat awry, lolling aside. The clerk walks approximately one hundred and one steps, by the skin of his teeth, and arrives at the bus stop. Invariably, he carries his umbrella with him, one never knows when it scatters. "There we are, Angela, almost on the bus, my dear" he mutters in his chin. The old clerk never looks around him, at the people waiting for the bus, frightened he might see odd creatures, pink or green haired, with pierced noses, ears, tattooed all over the face, neck, arms, or even the whole body. It gives him bad dreams, besides he realized it works as a bad omen. When a "city beast" appears in the morning, his whole day is ruined at work. Claims after claims, angry and frustrated plaintiffs waiting outside, his superior in bad mood.

At 5 o'clock sharp, Mr. Bittern closes the office and goes home, walking exactly one hundred and fifty five steps to the nearest bus station, tossing and murmuring. He gets on the bus and, in no time, he arrives home. The old clerk gets off the bus extremely careful, walking back home, dangling, muttering. The way back takes more time, usually, as the kids got out of school, playing outside. Mr. Bittern is a medium height man, his legs are thin, while his upper body is large and fat. He has a huge belly hanging over his belt and tends to walk leaned back, to keep his balance, otherwise his belly would pull him downwards. The man has an aquiline nose, which, when getting furious and nervous enough, could almost change its form into a bird's beak, while the eyes are twinkling under bushy, white eyebrows.

Two boys around eleven were outside, playing with their mobile phones. When they saw Mr. Bittern coming down the street, they started giggling. "There he comes, Mr. Birdie-Birdie". "Where?" "He comes towards us, staggering and panting like a steam-engine". "Hey, Georgie, don't come out, Mr. Birdie-Birdie is going to swallow you and you'll never be able to get out of his belly", one of them shouted to their younger neighbour. Little Georgie rushed back inside the house, screaming. They used that trick with the younger kids, to keep them away. Certainly, the size of Mr. Bittern's stomach, somehow entitled them to imagine such horrors.

As the old man approached, the boys began to caw like the bittern, with short guttural sounds "wua, wua, wua, wua",

96

combined with a slight, almost inaudible barking. The old clerk passed by them, gasping, ignoring them, stepping as quickly as he could, baked in his own swelter. Mr. Bittern was now at the middle of the distance, fifty steps more to take, when he observed a group of teenagers standing outside, bored, smoking, drinking out of cans, listening to music, laughing out loud. "I wish I could turn them into pigs", like Circe did, Mr. Bittern thought. *Wretched man, where are you off to, wandering the hills of an unknown island all alone? Your friends are penned in Circe's house, pigs in close-set sties. Have you come to free them? I tell you, you won't return, you'll end up like the rest.* He could avoid them going down the next street, where there were other teens, maybe worse than these. "Angie, when we were kids, we behaved, didn't we? Now, they are different". Mr. Bittern almost ran, he didn't even know how he got in front of the entrance, rummaging into his briefcase, atilt, turning its content inside out. He opened the door with a trembling hand, rushing inside, slamming the door behind, locking it, hastily. "We are home again, Angela, my dear, safe and sound", he said, dropping the briefcase on the floor, leaning against the wall, breathing in great difficulty.

Every night after the daily trip to work and back home, Mr. Bittern goes to sleep early, but curiously, wakes up awfully tired. He dreams the same dream, which seems to be repeating on and on, or, at least, that's the explanation he found for this unusual situation. He never told anybody about it - that's his best kept secret - he dreams that, after midnight, he turns into an odd bird, flying above the houses. His secret was safe, since no neighbours ever suspected it, maybe for the reason that turning into a common bird is not as dangerous as turning into a vampire or a wolf, to eat other people. It is just that, in his dreams, Mr. Bittern enjoyed to fly

9

freely, no matter it was raining or not, resting from time to time on a roof, then on another one, chirping onto various tree branch, here and there. As strange as it might sound, the young boys that live on the same street are regularly awakened by the noise made by a crazy bird on the roof, drumming the ceramic tiles and, sometimes, even their bedrooms' windows.

One night, somebody had insomnia, reading outside, in the garden. It was a stoned silence at that hour, one could hear the butterfly fluttering its wings. The nocturnal reader heard a strange noise and lifted his head, looking that direction. There is was, a huge bird, brown and beige, watching him with a man's head. The beak, especially, was a combination between a fountain pen and a steel bullet, shining relentlessly into the moonlight. It seemed to keep modifying its size and shape, growing into a rocket's nose cone. The late reader rubbed his eyes in shock, the hallucination didn't disappear, though. Quite contrarily, it started to talk: "Hi, I am Mr. Bitter ...", when the first beams of sun light appeared, making the strange creature, an amalgamation of human, avian, technical traits, disappear, leaving behind a brown feather. Mr. Bittern woke up in a pool of his own sweat.

# THE SHOW

*The murdered DO haunt their murderers, I believe*

The front door slammed over her hysterical screams, suddenly cut short, while Sliver pretended to be asleep, listening to the argument, without being obliged to intervene. She didn't agree on their daughter's choice to live with a man married to another woman, father to a little girl. The scandal repeated every time they saw each other, after the usual exchange of small talk, compliments and sweet words. He never expressed his opinion openly, annoying his wife, accusing him of complicity in the destruction of their daughter's life, proving that he does not care what happens to her. The daughter was immoral, totally like her father, from whom she inherited the weakness for the opposite sex, an immeasurable appetite for food, together with the shape of the mouth, of the teeth and the pronounced nose, rather an exacerbated pride and the tendency to mendacity. As her father, she was able to lie with a smile and a girlish voice thinned to make up incredible details, anointed with an unctuous smile, languorous glances, rhythmic beats of the thick eyelashes over dilated pupils.

The bathroom door was closed. In the next moment, he heard the water running. Sliver checked the mobile, his daughter's text message was received, telling him she went mad and things had to be discussed, she can no longer endure it, his help is really needed. The man remembered that many

9

times the daughter told him she feels like putting an end to her life. His heart went tighter, the mouth turned bitter, while he lay in bed, facing the ceiling, clenching his teeth and fists, rehearsing the plan made years ago, along with his confident and accomplice. The husband slightly winced hearing the thud, the eyelids throbbed over the eyeballs, breathing has accelerated and his body was filled with a creamy warmth, felt whenever sipping fresh coffee, in the office.

Finally alone, without her useless talk, without her face, image he couldn't get rid of, hanging on every eyelash, desperately, not to fall down into the abyss. "She has finally fallen", he told himself, keeping eyes closed, under the covers, alone in his room. Sliver made no movement, only the eyelids have slightly struggled. The man started to rhythmically count the seconds, calculating the minutes passed, until her weakened heart, an old, rusty clockwork, occupying unnecessary space on the wall, would cease to beat, not to be resuscitated ever again. The man numbered up to 300, five minutes have passed, it was high time to get up and tackle a worried face. The man picked up the white rubber gloves from the drawer, used to prepare the dose of medication for her, put them on, slowly opened the room's door and stepped cautiously on the dark hallway, counting the steps, decomposing them in centimetres. He stopped after three meters, listening tense, trying to detect any fizzle or residue of breathlessness. He began to walk slowly, again, with soft cat steps, wearing thick wool socks, which cushioned the creaks. He slipped on the floor like a ghost, reaching the two nearing doors, the bathroom and his wife's room.

Sliver hesitated a second, then slowly put his head inside the first door, she was not there. He grabbed the doorknob of the bathroom, pressed it gently, the water was still running.

His heart was beating fast, almost stifled with impatience. The man cracked the door slowly, millimetre by millimetre and saw her fallen down on the tiles, with a foot caught on the edge of the bathtub, hanging by the plastic shower curtain, with wet hair and glassy eyes. He approached and looked at her, inhaling the shower gel perfume slowly, with parted lips and eyes closed. Sliver opened his eyes, grabbed one hand, dragging the body out of the bathroom, towards her room. The corpse left behind thin streaks of water, while the swollen abdomen trembled hideously. He felt like puking. Brought a lime bath robe and dressed her, tied the belt over the abdomen and went to mop the traces of water on the floor. The man returned to the room and twirled her head and face in a thick, white towel. Rising back, he looked at the time displayed on the mobile phone screen, 14.15, and began to dial the emergency number. The operator replied and he communicated the prepared text: "My wife, suffering from congestive heart failure, filed at the C.F. Hospital, had a heart attack". He continued telling the address and hung up, remaining still, looking at her, while repeating a statement to give to the emergency crew.

For the first time in his life, he felt triumphant, powerful, domineering. It was her who was undermining his power from the start, making him lose control, desiring her young and beautiful body, causing him jealousy whenever other men coveted her. All those years of torture are over now, as she grew old and ugly, he became more self-possessed, exercising cold minded thinking. He calculated his every move like a mathematical problem, now he had only one step to take, most importantly, to seize all the wealth. His lips were stretched in a thin smile, the eyes narrowed, and his mind began to calculate the probabilities and variables as in a C++ application.

1

He opened the door, the emergency crew arrived quickly, in five minutes. He was quite amazed, stuttering almost imperceptibly, thinking how clever of him to secure a margin of extra five minutes. In his statement, he tried hard to squeeze a few tears and a sigh of pain through words. Actually, he was crying, because, in fact, he wasted his youth with that woman, the regrets of a life which seemed meaningless now. However, not too many tears were shed, nor he sighed too heavy, careful not to arouse suspicion. It was meant as an uncontrollable outburst of a man in distress, expressed with dignity.

In the emergency report, it was recorded: - CPR practice protocol. (35 min) to no avail. 14.55 declared deceased. Also, the report specifies: Reason for request: unconscious anamnesis: pac. found unconscious at home no vital signs present on the monitor - asystole – CPR protocol, manoeuvres, medication and treatment: atropine 3 mg. Adrenaline 6 mg., treatment at home: Furosemide, Tertensif, Digoxin, Sintrom, Aspacardin, Silymarin. Patient Status: 18-Dec. back ground. Manoeuvres / procedures: 13-oxygen, intubation 15-IOT without induction, 16-Ball, 21-FR: 14 ml, 22-FIO2 100% Print EKG, EKG-24, 25-Monit. EKG, intravenous access: 33 Periferic- No. cai: 1. Functions vital exam: Pupils 05-unreactive, 07-mydriasis, sputum obstructed airway, breathing 15-absent, absent peripheral pulse-19, P-27 where absent, absent murmur 37th, cardiac auscultation 44-absent 47 tegument - warm, 53-cyanotic, ap. digestive abd 59th. relaxed, vital functions takeover: 07-CR Stop, 10th at 14.21 Resuscitation 12- Failed death: 14.55.

The plan went according to the strategy, scrupulously put in place, leaving nothing to chance. Every night he could not sleep, and many have been in recent years, he analysed the possible or unexpected twists of the situation, any detail, no matter how insignificant could mess everything, being absolutely necessary to take into account any variable. After the emergency crew left, he texted his daughter, whom he previously advised to make herself seen in a public place, a parking if possible, where to be seen by as many people as possible. Everything was simple, given that she lived down town presently, in her partner's apartment. Then he dialled one of his acquaintances who had a funeral firm, announced the death and called for organizing funeral services. He was informed that he must descend to the city, to arrange for the registration of death. The man called the two sons, one located in the capital and another abroad, giving them the news, abruptly, in a few words, almost telegraphic. Then he took the car keys, the purse, the emergency report sheet and left the house, turning the key in the door, whose sound sealed closed a chapter of his life.

One thing slipped, though, but it wasn't his error, in the death certificate it was noted that the registration date was year 09, month X (October), day 18, in the upper left corner, while below in the body of the certificate, it was written month XI (November). This little vertical line worked like a nail stuck in his brain, he did not understand the mistake, as if implying premeditation. Anyway, he thought, perhaps no one will notice, who could be interested in an old retired woman, he realized he had no reason whatsoever to worry, calming himself, thinking about the prospects ahead. He was waiting for this moment for such a long time, and behold, it is here!

He gave orders to his brain, trained in self-suggestion since in college, when he had to memorize endless courses, during the exams session. He used to impose himself a draconian regime of sleepless nights, even without coffee, then he could not afford this luxury, coffee was only for the

1

privileged, and he was as poor as a church mouse. In faculty, she was beautiful, proud, wealthy, not looking at him and how much he wanted her to belong to him, to all of his colleagues envy. Since then, he made his plan to seize her, a wealthy, only child - had learned details from a friend of hers- possessing land and forest, a large barn, a yard full of animals and a big house with three spacious rooms, built by the hand of her father, a hardworking peasant, hardened in World War II. He was sure that it will not be easy with the soldier, yet he was certain that her mother would nibble at his hand.

He awoke from his memories, repositioning easily, just as an acrobat practising with elastic movements, he could not risk to become sentimental, although it might help to make him look sadder, overthrew. He slightly frowned the eyebrows, slowly arched his back, as if under an invisible weight, and left the corner of the lips to fall down. He was just like an actor about to enter the stage, acting in the show of his life, and the role had to be played perfectly, there was no chance of a prompter, nor rehearsals.

# A CIGARETTE BUTT

The raindrops were dripping on Mr. Buttoggs' face, lingering in the wrinkles of his skin, a labyrinth of lines, cuts and folds, slithering down his beard, neck, then on his left hand, damping the cigarette. Alistair's hand was clenched on the stub, bony, leaden and crouched like a scorched twig. It was pouring, the lightning flashing on his still body, thin and dry as a tattered cloth glove. The old man struggled to draw breath, ruckling and sniffing, coughing and spitting around. His breath slowly quenched, leaving him on the pavement, stuck with his back against the wall. Being a heavy drinker, nobody cared to check on him, considering he was sleeping after a spree. Next day, people passed by him, going to work, to school, into the park, shopping, finding Mr. Buttoggs in the same place, in a similar position. An old lady, who knew him for many years, stopped to say hello, but got no answer. She took a closer look and realized Mr. Buttoggs was not breathing anymore. The old woman stepped into the nearest store and asked the salesclerk to call the ambulance.

Waiting, bits of memories about him rushed into her mind. The old woman remembered Mr. Buttoggs as a young, handsome man, popular with the ladies of the times. He courted her assiduously, rivalling her future husband. Mr. Buttoggs was living the moment, applying the *carpe diem* principle, never worrying about the future, not even the next day. "All will get sorted, no reason to worry", he used to say. He went to lots of parties, drank, had fun, smoked, never fixing itself in a constant relationship with a woman. "Georgiana, you are the most beautiful girl I have ever met. Let's be together", he told her once. Next week, he forgot to come where they planned to meet. After a few days, she saw him walking with another woman, as if nothing would have happened between them. She did not understand what was going on, felt hurt, then realized he is strange and it was better for her to forget him. Since then, she saw him a few times at some parties, invariably with the cigarette in his hand, his hair slimy, the shirt's collar marked with streaks of dirt. The cigar was burning in his hand like a spark of hellfire, the devil's incense, squeezing the life out of him, bit by bit. It was as if the cigar was never put out, maintaining itself lit with his own breath, extorting it slowly and securely. The cigar was always in his hand or mouth, burning red, dissipating, enveloping everything in a cloud of smoke.

Soon, she got married and settled down with her husband, racking their brains with the house mortgage, the jobs and their child, while Mr. Buttoggs remained a bachelor. "I am still on the market", he used to say, laughing. Gradually, the women he got out with became more vulgar, uglier, drinking, smoking, toothless, ungraceful, staggering on the streets, laughing, screaming or crying hysterically, stumbling and falling over each other. They grew to be the clowns of the town, Mr. Buttoggs and his Buttogins, almost Dickensian characters. One day, he saw him begging on the street, staring at her like a beaten dog. He didn't seem to know who she was. The woman felt sorry for him and gave him ten pounds. He was unrecognizable, like a wild animal, devoid of reason. Georgiana was curious to see what he was going to do with the money. In less than five minutes, he stood up and entered the nearest Booze and News convenience store, getting out with a bottle of alcohol in one hand and a lit cigarette in the other. The ordinary cigarette, his curse, his damnation. Alistair Buttogs was almost a skeleton in rags, dangling, crashing into the passers-by.

The salesclerk told her that the ambulance is expected to arrive in any moment. She went out and waited outside, a few steps away from the corpse. The medical crew asked her about the dead person: "Who is he? Is he her relative? Does he have any kinsfolk, caregivers?" They found no documents with him, deciding to deliver the dead body to the morgue. There, they put a label on his toes, deposited him in the positive temperature cold chamber for a few weeks, awaiting for identification. Unidentified, they moved him in the negative temperature cold chamber, between -10 and – 50°C, for dissections and medical experiments. After a year, they decided to cremate him. What was left from the corpse burned in the furnace, disintegrating in less than an hour. Finally, Mr. Buttoggs became a handful of ashes on the bottom of a giant ashtray.

That night, Georgiana dreamt about a fire bursting on the street, quickly reaching her roof and in no time, her house was on fire. The dense smoke caused her to faint, trapping her on the floor, while the fire spread rapidly, coming down, consuming everything in its way. Georgiana felt the blazes on the skin, warming her gently, as the summer evening sun in July, or cutting her, cold as a steel knife edge forgotten in the freezer. *The burning death that turns to ice.* Her breathing stopped for a few seconds, but the woman finally woke up, coughing brutally, blinded by the hot sunshine, drained in the room through the velvet curtains.

# THE GOLDEN LOTUS

*There were the Hortensia flowers that confer Eternal Life, Flowers of the Sacred Cloud, and the Fusang Plant; flowers that never faded, blossoming so luxuriantly that the eyes could scarce bear to dwell on them*

Once upon a time, there lived a man named Ci-Hao Lao Si. He was esteemed by everyone, being regarded as rich, and was always welcomed at the king's court. Ci-Hao had many children, houses, jewels and gems, however, in the depths of his soul, he was not satisfied. He was in search of, nor did he not know what, but he felt that he still needed something more, to be completely happy. He did not have peace and ran all day long, like a ghost. Now he was here and then he was gone the next moment, so that the people, amazed beyond measure, called him the Phantom. On his way, he accommodated at all the inns and teahouses, no matter how humble, engaging in trade and politics. He listened, though rarely spoke and quietly eavesdropped off by the dark corners. And he was generous, not backing away from anything when something caught his interest. Wherever he went, he was interested in most unusual things: was there, somewhere, a charming bird coveted by the Grand Emperor Go Sanjo-Tenno himself? Ci-Hao purchased it quickly and sent it to the palace. Heard about the most beautiful woman in distant lands? He travelled up there to bring her home. The most expensive silk, the purest gold, the finest porcelain, Ci-Hao bought them all. He kept some of them, offering the others to the noblest samurais. "Ci-Hao collects rare things", people of the land began to speak and rumours started to spread.

One summer, he was wandering from village to village. Unexpectedly, a lightning streaked the sky as violently from one side to another, with deafening thunders. Ci-Hao was in Edo, in a petty tearoom. He was sipping tea, satisfied with the last purchase, a roll of silk in most beautiful colours, it looked like the sunset was reflected in it, changing its waters after the eye of the beholder. It was of an unparalleled beauty, indeed. Two poor old people were drinking sake on the side-lines, whispering. Ci-Hao harked and vaguely heard something about a golden lotus. The man became very attentive, his nostrils flared like a stallion's in a mad race. Ci-Hao offered drinks for everybody, rivers of sake flew over, the most beautiful geishas played the Shamisen. The two old men stated that, back to their childhood village, an old monk told them the golden lotus legend. Every few thousand years, on the high peak of the Mount Fuji-Yama, a golden lotus makes its appearance, shining brighter than the sun and all the emperor's diamonds, altogether. Nobody has ever seen it, but legends say that a poor, young monk would have reached it, long time ago. The old monk said that the golden lotus belonged to Buddha Shakya Muni himself and only the Enlightened Maitreya, "Buddha-who-will-come", could be able to pick it up.

From that day on, Ci-Hao has lost his mind. He could not drink, nor eat, he would get no sleep, no matter how much he tried. He wandered from village to village, inquiring about the golden lotus. Nobody knew anything. He almost lost hope when, after twelve months of wandering, an old woman told him that she heard a Zen monk talking about a golden lotus. Ci-Hao hit the road, reached Yu-Hang temple and asked of the wise monk Siu Lao. In a few minutes, an old

1

monk made his entrance, fixing Ci-Hao with piercing eyes and handed him an old mouldy scroll, leaving the room without a word. With precipitated movements, Ci-Hao had the roll unfolded, smiling broadly. He got Mount Fuji-Yama's map, containing the cave where the Golden Lotus was last seen. He left immediately, making preparations for the trip, hiring attendants, carriers and samurais. The string of people began to climb wild mountains, passing over bottomless abysses, impetuous rivers, fighting with giant bears and bloody wolves.

After several weeks, they climbed half a mountain, Ci-Hao was satisfied, all was going according to his plans. That night he had a strange dream - a woman or a goddess whispered something into his ear, smiling bewitchingly. He woke up distressed beyond measure and rushed his people on the road, at dawn. A few weeks passed again and it seemed they span in circles, no matter how they walked, they could not climb the other half of the mountain. People were frightened, some of them heard odd laughter, ghostly whispers in the glades and started to believe that creepy demons came out of hell to haunt them. One by one, they gave up the travel, returning home. In four months, Ci-Hao was left alone. Without help, and no food, climbing the mountain paths, he lost his mind, running with his hair dishevelled, eating roots and fungi, drinking water from rivers or ponds. He often dropped almost lifeless to the ground, tormented by pain and despair. Then, the mysterious woman appeared in his dreams, smiling charmingly. After a while, Ci-Hao began to speak to foxes and birds, once it seemed like a bear said something. He climbed and climbed, tireless, driven either by a blinding rage, or by the call of a bird.

One night, the goddess took him by the hand and brought him into a dense forest, where his eyesight was struck by a blinding light. The man rubbed his eyes, noticing that if he closed his eyelids, he could look that way without being hurt, slowly, while the brightness increased and godlike music could be softly heard. There, seated on the golden lotus, the dream goddess waited for him, smiling charmingly. Ci-Hao picked her hand and plunged into the light, while seeing his arms and legs disappear, the whole body molten, becoming music and light. Since then, never was heard anything about Ci-Hao, some say he went to the land of the gods, now called Maha -Vairochana, others believe that a demon captured him in the inferno.

The wise monk Siu Lao recorded the following text in

*The Golden Leaf of the Enchanting Days: In the seventeenth year of the Great Emperor Go-Sanjo Tenno, Ci-Hao, much beloved servant of the enlightened Emperor, while in royal mission on the Mount Fuji-Yama, was attacked by a wild boar as never seen before, with two huge fangs on every side of the muzzle. The boar made him small-shreds.*

# THE PUBLIC LIBRARY

Fergie had a school project to prepare at home, for which she was expected to do research online and at the library. Therefore, she decided to walk to the Public Library, holding her umbrella, almost carried away by the strong gusts of wind. It rained cats and dogs and the water streamed down the pavement in great fury, washing the dirt. It was the period of floods, lots of houses were inundated in Scotland and the Northern part of England, people had to be relocated, it was mud all over and the girl felt sad and sorry for the victims, times seem to be changing lately. The girl got to the entrance of the old Public Library, inaugurated at the beginning of the 20th century, a high building covered with ivy on the front and back side, as well as laterally. It had a wide, high entrance, reached after climbing large stairs, leaving her an impression of coldness, due to the grey-white stone and concrete used for construction.

Above the entrance, there was a mysterious emblem on the triangular frontispiece, sustained by two gross, circular poles. Fergie entered the building, stepping towards the history of religion shelves. Reading about Christianism, she found out that it was finally recognised as a legal religion in the Roman Empire by the Emperor Constantin and his mother, Elena in 313 A.D. After less than one hundred years, worshipping other gods became illegal in the Roman Empire. In pagan religions, so many and so diverse that almost pulverized the Roman Empire and other former civilizations, nobody truly ever knew how many gods and goddesses existed. Fergie read about cruel human sacrifice rituals in old pagan customs and got terrified. Economically, former pagan societies were based on the exploitation of human slaves, men, women and children, prisoners from other countries.

A famous slave was Spartacus, forced to fight as a gladiator in the arena, to entertain the masses and the aristocracy. *You'd be surprised what profound ignorance there is here and there about, concerning the wars of Spartacus. Now see here, this young lady, she asks me, is that one Spartacus?* Another famous slave was Joseph, sold by his brothers to serve as a slave in Egypt. Good-looking, educated and endowed with a special gift of interpreting dreams, highly appreciated in those times, Joseph succeeded to gain the rights of a free man, consolidating his position in the high-society. He knew how to organize the food resources for the whole state of Egypt and convinced the authorities he is able to manage the state affairs. *"Here comes that dreamer!" they said to each other. "Come now, let's kill him and throw him into one of these cisterns and say that a ferocious animal devoured him. Then we'll see what comes of his dreams."*

The first centuries were difficult for the Christians, their religion being hated by the pagans. They used to punish the Christians, mainly poor people, vibrating at the idea of social justice, providential reward for kind people, in real life and after death. The Christian religion taught people to be tolerant, understanding, merciful and generous to each other. Yet, the first Christians were killed in horrible ways, burned alive, crucified, eaten by wild animals in the arena. Most of them are sanctified now for their inner strength and the extraordinary courage they had to fight against the injustice, being punished with terrible ordeals Their blood stained the Earth for millennia, absorbed into the layers, evaporated into

1

the sky, drawn by others into their lungs, diluted into the waters, drained under the stones, turned into lions' cells. *Martyrs being tortured in the following ways: A. Hang from the wooden horse and scorched with the flames of the torches; B. Suspended by the feet from a pulley and tortured with torches.* One of them was St. Agnes[1], executed at the age of twelve or thirteen, an innocent child born in 291 AD, killed in 303, a few years before the recognition of the Christian religion in the Roman Empire.

The girl remained silent for a few seconds, trying hard not to let the tears flow, staring into the distance. She got out, where the rain had turned into a storm, blinding lightnings and deafening thunders tore the sky, merely a piece of paper. When she got home, Fergie was shivering, soaked wet. She took a hot shower, put her Disney pyjama on and sipped a hot tea, thinking about the Noah's Great Flood, her grandmother told her about. She also knew about the pre-Christian Atlantis Civilization, which completely disappeared into the waters, thousands of years ago. Fergie suddenly heard a strong thud on the floor, a book fell down the shelf. She picked the book up and read the title, *The Decline of the West* by Oswald Spengler, given to her by her grandmother. The girl opened it, curiously, reading: *Woman, as Time, is that for which there is history at all.* She closed it, then reopened it, reading again: *"Mankind" however, has no aim, no idea, no plan, any more than the family of butterflies or orchids. "Mankind" is a zoological expression, or an empty word.* She put it back on the shelf and went back to bed, drained of power.

That night, the girl slept agitated, tossing and turning around. She dreamt about a strange guy, whose face seemed blurred, only the eyes could be seen, blue, burning in two separate fires, surrounding the irises. She saw this man lifting

---

[1] http://www.stagnescathedral.org/Our%20Parish/Patroness.html

the lids from the stone tubes, at each side of the Public Library's entrance, which contained two huge rolls of a very old, valuable manuscript, hidden inside. The manuscripts were traversed by two long red crosses on each side, giving the impression it would burst in fire, while the religious icons seemed to move, like videos projected on a screen.

# A FIERCE BATTLE

She ran into the woods, outside the village, where she thought she could take cover, but the hideous monster followed her, howling and punching his chest with the huge fists, wreathed in fire. It had two curvy horns on his head, a huge eye in the middle of the forehead, spitting fire out of his mouth. Two black wings opened, allowing him to fly in wide space, however he couldn't do it there or downtown, among high storied buildings. Evy had to reach the nearest city and mingle with other people, the monster would never come there. Angry because she escaped, the furious creature stroke and crushed everything in its way, making the earth quake. "You are so small!", his voice thundered. "I could crush you like a bug. Ha ha ha ha ha ha! ...", his voice echoed all over. Frightened, she stumbled on a log and fell down a slope into a dark, dense side of the forest, never walked before.

Evy could feel the earth trembling under her feet, moving so fast she never thought she could. The trees were huge and she couldn't see the light because of their thick crowns. Her heart was throbbing like a jungle drum, she was wounded, blood streamed on her hands, still she held the sword and the shield tightly, as if it was a part of her body. The girl's feet were sore, she breathed heavily and almost hit her head on a trunk. She could feel the monster's heat behind her, while the beast snatched the trees out, flinging them towards the village. She stumbled again, fell down and screamed, with the left leg broken.

The girl crawled behind a giant tree, closed her eyes trying to keep calm, reaching for the magic silver amulet, whispering the mystic formula. The monster was close now, burning the bark of the trees and the fallen leaves with his flames. Frightened animals roared, disappearing into the mist. Evy could hear distant calls, the heat became almost unbearable, when she saw the huge claw reaching for her. She screamed, shut down the computer and got out into the sunshine, to meet her friends in the neighbourhood park. There, she stood on a wooden bench, texting them, still thinking about the fierce battle led with Balor of the Evil Eye, feeling her heart beating like a drum.

Among the trees, near the brook, she spotted a man staring at her, dressed in jeans and a brown jacket. The guy realized she saw him and walked towards her bench. Alarmed, she tried to stand up and step away, but she couldn't, her feet were jellylike. The man kept coming her way, she could see he was dark-eyed and dark-haired. She looked around, nobody was there, only a woman on the other side of the park, leaving with a dog. She took the phone, dialled her mother's number, telling her that she is alone in the park and a strange man comes towards her. "Go away, run quickly, run!", the mother told her. A police car siren was heard on the street and the man stopped instantly, going back to the trees. The girl arrived on the alley again and saw her friends coming. Nervous and frightened, she told them about the odd man hidden among the trees. They went down the street, turned the corner to the fast food restaurant, catching a glimpse of the man, still there. One of the girls took a photo, zooming the image, a quite clear image, a bit blurred on the margins, but good enough to record the garments and the distinguishing marks. She instantly sent the image to the other girls and Evy forwarded it to her mother.

1

The group of girls arrived at the restaurant, ordered the meals and ate, chatting about the unusual occurrence. One of them looked out of the large window and saw the man standing there, watching them. She screamed and all the girls turned their heads, seeing him while he stepped away. The girls called their families and cars came to take them home, one by one. Next day, Evy thought she glimpsed the same man outside the school entrance, with the brown jacket, staring at the girls. Some of them wore short skirts, high heels, make-up and décolletage and the man used a small phone to take pictures of the most attractive girls. She called her mom to take her home, waiting in the library till she arrived. Her mother came and announced the school reception there is a suspicious man following the girls. A guardian was called, being told to go outside and check on the described person. Seeing the guardian coming his way, the brown jacket man got into his car and drove away. The school alerted the police and a portrait of the man, together with a description and a stay-away report was given to all the students. Evy did not see him again, yet she has never forgotten the scare, being careful when going out on the street or in the park, taking care not to be alone. She always had a fully charged phone with her and gave up wearing provocative clothes and make up. After all, she is just a 13 years old girl, even though she looks mature.

# Contents

1

**Casa Cărţii de Ştiinţă**
Director: Mircea Trifu
Fondator: dr. T. A. Codreanu
Tehnoredactare computerizată: Alexandra Blendea

Tiparul executat la Casa Cărţii de Ştiinţă
400129 Cluj-Napoca; B-dul Eroilor nr. 6-8
Tel./fax: 0264-431920
www.casacartii.ro; e-mail: editura@casacartii.ro

www.ingramcontent.com/pod-product-compliance
Lightning Source LLC
Chambersburg PA
CBHW060642130626
46555CB00002B/916